For more than forty years,
Yearling has been the leading name
in classic and award-winning literature
for young readers.

Yearling books feature children's
favorite authors and characters,
providing dynamic stories of adventure,
humor, history, mystery, and fantasy.

Trust Yearling paperbacks to entertain,
inspire, and promote the love of reading
in all children.

OTHER YEARLING BOOKS YOU WILL ENJOY

tall tales

KAREN DAY

A Yearling Book

Published by Yearling, an imprint of Random House Children's Books
a division of Random House, Inc., New York

This is a work of fiction. Names, characters, places, and incidents either are the product
of the author's imagination or are used fictitiously. Any resemblance to actual persons,
living or dead, events, or locales is entirely coincidental.

Visit us on the Web! www.randomhouse.com/kids
Educators and librarians, for a variety of teaching tools, visit us at
www.randomhouse.com/teachers

The Library of Congress has cataloged the hardcover edition of this work as follows:
Day, Karen
Tall tales / Karen Day.
p. cm.
Summary: Sixth-grader Meg Summers and her family move to a new state every few years,
her alcoholic father trying to get a fresh start, but when they land in Indiana and Meg
finally makes a real friend and eventually begins to talk about her family's problems,
they all find the strength to try to change their destiny.
ISBN 978-0-375-83773-9 (trade) — ISBN 978-0-375-93773-6 (glb)
[1. Alcoholism—Fiction. 2. Family problems—Fiction. 3. Family life—Indiana—Fiction.
4. Friendship—Fiction. 5. Schools—Fiction. 6. Indiana—Fiction.] I. Title.
PZ7.D3316Tal 2007
[Fic]—dc22
2006035242

ISBN: 978-0-375-83774-6 (pbk.)
Reprinted by arrangement with Wendy Lamb Books
Printed in the United States of America
November 2008
10 9 8 7 6 5 4 3 2 1
First Yearling Edition

For David, Dylan, Emma, and Elizabeth

Chapter 1

I want to make a friend.

But as I stand in the entrance of the lunchroom, panic ringing in my ears, all I think is Here we go again. New town. New school. Same old feeling.

Teddy thinks the worst part about a new school is being introduced in every class that first day. He hates being stared at. But when my English teacher introduced me today, I walked to my seat smiling as if I'd won an Academy Award.

At lunch, though, you don't have an assigned seat and a teacher to introduce you.

I look around the room. There's a table of happy, peppy blond girls by the milk shake machine. A group of boys sits behind them. They are loud and cheer when someone throws a chocolate milk carton at the girls. Right in front of me a girl wearing a hoodie is dunking chocolate chip cookies into milk.

Aunt Jane said I should find a table, walk up, and introduce myself. She said people would respect that I'm so friendly. *Hi. I'm Meg and I'm in sixth grade. We just moved here from Michigan.*

But now that idea seems impossible. What if they laugh at me? Ignore me?

I take my turkey sandwich into the bathroom and sit in a stall with the door closed and eat. I read the graffiti on the wall. There is a whole story going on. Jennifer Somebody was going with Joey until Roxanne went out with him while Jennifer was at Cedar Point. Now everyone hates Roxanne.

I stay in the stall until the bell rings. As I walk out, a group of girls charges in. I recognize them from the peppy blond table. One of the girls stares at me.

"You're new," she says. "You're in my social studies class, second period."

I can't think of anything to say, I'm so surprised. Then one of the girls grabs her and they rush out the door, giggling. But she waves goodbye.

Wouldn't it be funny if that girl and I ended up as friends?

I look at myself in the mirror and smile and watch my shoulders rise as I take a deep breath. I feel, briefly, as if I can do anything.

At the Boston airport before I got on the plane to come back here two weeks ago, Aunt Jane grabbed me by my shoulders and said, "You have to take charge of your life. Your father isn't going to help you."

I know what she thinks of Dad. She tried to get me to talk about him the entire week I visited her and Uncle Terry. But I don't talk to her about Dad anymore. I don't talk about him with anyone except Mom, Teddy, and Abby.

"You have to choose your own destiny." That was the last thing she said to me.

Destiny. It sounds so grand and exciting. Powerful. Limitless. I walk down the hall and stop in front of the library. I'm feeling my destiny as I read a sign on the door, about the first meeting for the school newspaper club. Since I want to be a writer, I should go to the meeting. We'll see.

A girl with pigtails and braces stands next to me, reading the sign. Will she be in the club? She glances at me. Here is my chance. I take a deep breath.

"Hi. I'm Meg. I just moved here. I'm a sixth grader."

She looks me up and down.

"We moved here from Michigan."

She looks at me like Michigan is the most boring place in the world. Then she glances over my shoulder. My knees begin to shake. I *have* to say something.

"Before that we were in Tasmania. That's an island off Australia. My family is from Australia. My dad is a doctor. He worked with the natives and we lived in tents for the past three years. We had to come back because he caught a disease and lost fifty pounds and we needed this special medicine that you can't get in Tasmania."

The girl's mouth drops open, and I can count the fillings in her teeth. Then two of her friends appear and the three of them walk off.

I feel my destiny take off down the hall after them.

Chapter 2

I'm twelve years old, with brown eyes and brown hair. I'm a straight-A student. My sister, Abby, is seven and my brother, Teddy, is fourteen. I love Oreos, anything about Australia, and animals, but Dad won't let us get a pet until we prove we're "responsible."

These are the things I should write about when my English teacher, Mrs. Hollis, tells us to write a paragraph about ourselves to share with the class.

Instead, I write about how I almost died of meningitis last year and how a helicopter rushed me to a hospital in Chicago and how this wonderful lady doctor gave me a last-minute blood transfusion that saved my life. When it's my turn to read, Mrs. Hollis sits on the edge of her desk. When I finish, her eyes are wide open.

Everyone stares at me as I sit, and I like that, even though I feel guilty about what I've written. When the bell rings, I dash into the hall and on to gym. Pretty soon I forget about that guilty feeling because I don't want to think about my paragraph as lying. I'm not exactly sure why I say the things I do.

This is our second time living in Indiana. I was born here, but I don't remember it, because we moved to Illinois when I was only two years old. After that we moved to Michigan, to Ohio, back to Michigan, and now to Indiana again.

We live in Lake Haven, the Town o' Lakes, as the sign says when you first come into town. Within the city limits there are seven lakes. One is called Clear Lake, although I don't know why because it's filled with lily pads. Our last town, St. Joe, sits right on Lake Michigan. Now, *that* is a lake.

Before dinner I stand by the side of the house and look across the street to the other houses in the neighborhood. They're all pretty much the same—one story, brick, gray roofs. The closer you get to town, the tighter they're squeezed together. But if you look the other way, through the backyard, all you see are cornfields.

I stand there and turn my head. Country, town. Country, town. Country, town. And there I am, smack in between.

The whole time, I breathe in something horrible, like someone has poured rotten eggs into a fire.

"What's that awful smell?" I ask when Dad comes home from work.

He takes a breath. "The foundry. I'm so used it, I don't even smell it anymore."

I don't think I'll ever get used to it.

Chapter 3

Today after school Teddy hit a rock over the house with his baseball bat and made a two-inch crack in the windshield of Mom's car.

Now all we can do is wait.

Teddy tells us it was an accident. But Mom says it doesn't matter. Dad is going to "hit the ceiling." So now Teddy stands in the corner, his hands jammed in his pockets. I try to read from my history book, but all I really do is watch everyone.

Things had been going okay. The move, the unpacking. Yesterday Dad came home from work talking about his new job. This time will be different, he said. But now he's going to be mad at Teddy; this is just the kind of thing to set him off again.

"He's here," Abby says from the window. My throat tightens. I look out the window, but it's only a repair truck turning around in the driveway. Now we're back to our positions, Teddy in the corner, Mom and Abby at the window, and me, watching.

Last year Dad went five months without drinking. Then Mom forgot to pay the car insurance, and Dad saw the cancellation letter and blew up. Yelling. Screaming.

Drinking.

"He's here," Abby says.

When Dad comes in, he sits in a chair and takes off his yellow work boots. His hands are thick and dark, with black hair that covers his fingers and the tops of his hands. His socks stick to his feet as he peels them off. "Ah, that's better." But it's not until after Mom hands him coffee that I see in his eyes how it will be today and how I should feel.

Mom stands behind him and kneads his shoulders. He closes his eyes and smiles.

"Teddy hit a rock with his bat and put a crack in the windshield," Mom says softly. "But I'm sure the insurance will cover it."

The smile drops off Dad's face. He swears under his breath and stands and intentionally bumps into Teddy on his way to the living room. He sits in his chair and opens the newspaper. I stare at him, holding my breath. Abby takes my hand.

"It was an accident," Teddy says. Tears fill his eyes.

"You want to pay our insurance premiums? You know how much insurance costs a year? Huh? Christ, you're crying again?"

"I'm not crying!" Teddy squeezes back his tears.

"Crybaby." Dad buries his head in the paper.

Teddy bites his lip; his shoulders shake. But when he sees me watching him, he storms out of the house. I turn back to Dad. Hate burns across my forehead.

Later I find Teddy in the backyard, hitting dirt clumps into the cornfield with his bat. On our last night in

Michigan, Teddy and his best friends, Pete and Harris, burned their initials into the bat with Pete's wood-burning kit. Now I can't see the initials under the dirt stains.

Teddy knows I'm here, but he won't look at me. I want to talk, but lately he doesn't seem to like anything I say to him.

"We need to be patient with him," I say finally. Mom says Dad has a Dr. Jekyll and Mr. Hyde personality. Charming and fun when he's sober, and nasty and miserable when he's drunk. We need to help him, she always says.

"Oh yeah?" Teddy asks. A dirt clump explodes in the air above us. "Patient with what? What's his excuse now? He's not drinking. So why is he such a jerk?"

Maybe Dad has three personalities. There's also this crappy in-between state where he wants to drink. He's so on edge you don't know what he'll do.

I want to help. I know how sensitive Teddy is. But I also know he has a terrible temper. "At least Dad isn't drinking, right? And you didn't get punished."

Teddy's face is red, and his eyebrows come together. He rears back like he's going to smash the nearby tree with his bat. But he touches the bark with the tips of his fingers. Then he hurls the bat into the cornfield and stalks off into the house.

Just before dark I find the bat wedged between two rows of corn. I bring it back to the garage and put it in a safe place for him, next to the rakes and shovels.

Chapter 4

Today Abby and I meet a girl who moved into one of the new houses down the street. She has curly red hair, just like Brianna, my friend from last year. We all get our bikes and ride through the neighborhood. When Abby points to our house, the girl pulls into our driveway and leans her bike against Dad's truck. She wants to go inside.

"Better not," I say. "My brother's pet boa constrictor got loose in the house a while ago. We still can't find him."

"Your brother has a pet snake?"

"Yeah. He got it last year on an expedition in the rain forest. It's ten feet long."

She hightails it out of there, quick as can be. And that's the end of that.

"Teddy doesn't have a snake." But Abby tilts her head and looks at me, as if she wants to make sure. When she wrinkles her nose, her freckles all bunch together.

"I know." I don't often say this kind of thing in front of her. I glance at Dad's truck, and then Abby does, too.

"Maybe she can come back when Dad isn't home," Abby says.

"Maybe." But I know she'll never come again. Here was an opportunity to make a friend. But we can't chance it with Dad around.

We go to our bedroom. Abby colors and I think about school. This is the first time all three of us are in separate schools. I miss seeing one of them in the halls or in the lunchroom. I miss seeing anyone I know.

Last year Brianna and I ate lunch together every day. Lots of times we just sat there, not saying a word. Brianna was nice but really quiet. This morning when Aunt Jane called, she told me that she and her best friend talk every single day. They're soul mates. Aunt Jane tells her things she's never told anyone else. I'd like to have a friend like that.

Today this girl whose locker is next to mine asked if I was new. She told me her name. Roxanne. Roxanne from the bathroom stall?

Chapter 5

On certain days you can smell the foundry, depending on the wind. If the wind is blowing from the north, not only can you smell it, but you can also hear it. Grinding and humming and banging. Tonight we smell the foundry the second we open the front door.

"Ew, gross," Abby says as we get into the car with Mom. We're on our way to pick up Dad at work. The closer we get, the worse the smell. We roll up the windows and Mom jacks up the air-conditioning. Then we sit outside the foundry, freezing and waiting, but at least the stink isn't so bad.

Towdan Castings sits close to the street and stretches over four blocks. Three huge doors the size of our garage open to the street, and you can see big fires and smoke coming out of these machines. The cement is caked with dirt and ashes, and I can't take my eyes off a huge cauldron full of red and blue flaming liquid.

Dad told me what a casting is, how they pour liquid metal into huge molds that form a frame, or casting, for the outside of engines. But it's hard to imagine what that looks like. These engines must be a lot bigger than Dad's model plane engines.

A huge burst of white steam shoots out of a machine. My heart leaps, and for a second I imagine the machine coming to life and reaching out with its long pipes and grabbing me and swallowing me. I squeeze my eyes shut and grab on to the car seat.

When I open my eyes, I see someone walking toward us through the haze, and then I realize it's Dad. He's usually in the office, but today he must have worked with the machines because when he sits in the car I smell burning metal. Something black is stuck under his nails. He's smiling. He's always happy when he does stuff with his hands.

At dinner Dad says his boss told everyone at a meeting how Dad had made this really smart decision about something or other. He saved the foundry tons of money.

"I run a tight ship," Dad says. "This boss, he's the real deal. He's okay."

Usually Dad hates his bosses. Management people are fat and soft, he says.

"I knew this was going to be a good move." Mom spoons some mashed potatoes onto Dad's plate, then hers, and passes the bowl to me.

Dad smiles, wrinkles his nose, and shakes his finger in the air. "You need to learn to get along with other people, *Bob*." His voice is high-pitched and twangy, and he makes it sound as if he's speaking through his nose. He's imitating his old boss, Mr. Reilly.

Mom bursts out laughing, and then we all do, too. Even Teddy smiles. I know he's still angry about the other night, but he loves Dad's imitations.

"Do Mr. Higgins!" Abby yells. "Do Mr. Higgins!"

"No," Dad says. But he smiles.

"Yes, Mr. Higgins! *Please?*" Abby is bouncing in her chair now.

"Oh, okay." Dad stands, shakes out his shoulders, and hunches over as he walks. "Where is that goldarn kitty? He's around here somewhere. Here, little kitty-cat."

His voice is deep yet jumps when he says *kitty,* just like Mr. Higgins, our old neighbor. Dad even looks like him, stooped over and searching the floor the way Mr. Higgins searched his yard. We're all laughing, even Teddy now.

I don't know how he changes his voice, his body like that. It's almost as if he becomes a different person, that's how real it seems.

"Do Fiona Wright," Mom says.

"Aren't you tired of old Fiona?" Dad rolls up his sleeves.

"No!" Abby and I say together.

Fiona Wright was a cafeteria worker at the plant where Mom and Dad met. Mom told us she first saw Dad when he'd stand during lunch breaks, with his wild, long hair and holey jeans, and imitate Fiona. She thought it was the funniest thing she'd ever seen.

Dad breathes and then talks in a voice that's scratchy and deep yet girl-like at the same time. "Try the chipped beef. Made it myself yesterday. With my bare hands."

Abby laughs so hard that she doubles over in her chair. Then Dad does Mickey Mouse, Bill Clinton, and Barbra Streisand. We tell jokes. We talk and laugh.

This is the kind of dinner regular families have.

Chapter 6

"I hate this." Teddy slaps his math book closed.

Abby glances at him but then goes back to her drawing. Teddy opens his closet door and stares into the mirror that hangs on the inside.

I know school isn't as easy for him as it is for me. But something else is wrong, or at least different. What? "Are you going to play baseball here?"

Teddy shrugs.

"When will you hang up your *Star Wars* posters?" I ask. Usually that's the first thing he does after we move. Darth Vader above his bed. Han Solo above his desk.

"I don't care about *Star Wars*." Teddy sounds tired. "Besides, why bother?"

"Can I have your posters?" Abby asks.

"Sure."

Ever since I can remember, Abby and I have come to Teddy's room after dinner to play and talk and do our homework. When we were little we made tents with his blankets and pretended we were on a ship. He'd stand at his bureau and shoot plastic balls at us from the cannons on his Playmobil pirate ship.

15

"Hole in the stern!" Then he'd dive back into our ship. *"We're gonna shipwreck!"*

Now Teddy says we're too old for this. And since we moved here last month, he doesn't even talk much anymore.

"Dad likes his job," I say. Maybe we won't have to move again. Then Teddy could think about what else he wants to put on his walls.

"That's what he said last time." Teddy lies in bed and stares at the ceiling. "A couple months later everything was bad again."

"But maybe this time will be different." I believe it. Mom says that when Teddy was little, Dad went for years without drinking. He could change. He can do it because he's really smart. Uncle Terry says he was the smartest in the family when they grew up.

Mom calls it "the smarts." She says I've got it, too. Last year when Aunt Jane and Uncle Terry visited, Dad recited a poem about Paul Revere. He knew it all even though he hadn't thought about it in thirty years. Uncle Terry says he has a photographic memory.

When you're smart like that, you can do anything. That's what Aunt Jane says.

Teddy looks at the picture Abby is drawing.

"It needs a unicorn," she says. This is like all the pictures she draws lately—a castle, a thunderstorm, a princess hanging out a turret window, a mean fire-breathing dragon hiding under the water in the moat. The unicorn has to be a flying unicorn who rescues the princess. "Teddy, please?"

16

"I don't feel like it," Teddy says. "Besides, look at how big the dragon is. You think a little unicorn can save her?"

"Teddy, it has to!" Abby pouts.

"All right." He swings his legs over the side of the bed. Abby jumps up and leans across his lap as he draws. Zip, he's finished, and he hands the notebook back to her. He ruffles the top of her blond hair before lying back down. She frowns.

The unicorn isn't as good as the ones he usually draws. Its legs are too short. Its horn looks like a pig's snout. She opens her mouth.

"I'll help," I say. We know I can't draw, but Abby smiles and hands me her picture.

Chapter 7

The next day is Friday. After dinner I go with Dad to the field next to the school. We wear shorts and T-shirts and ride with the windows of the truck wide open. He tells me about the dives and turns his planes do. He tells me the same thing every time, but I don't mind.

At the field I lie in the grass and watch the planes soar above me. I'm the only one who will watch Dad fly. Teddy gets mad because Dad won't let him fly a plane on his own, and Abby says it's boring.

"Watch this," Dad yells. I sit up. The sky is dusky blue. The trees are still and the air smells like fresh dirt. He makes a plane do three diving circles. I hold my ears as it whines above me. A group of boys stops their football game and looks up, too.

Dad lands the plane on the baseball diamond, and the boys run toward it.

"Get away from that!" Dad starts off after them, his thin legs kicking up behind him. Within minutes he's overrun them, and they all stand over the plane. I hold my breath. Will he yell? Lose his temper? I'm too far away to hear what they're saying.

Then one of the boys laughs, and Dad slaps him on

the shoulder. Sweat breaks out across my upper lip, and I close my eyes and wipe my face with my hand. When I look up, I see them all crouched over the plane. For a moment I can't tell which one is Dad.

Later, on the way home, he slouches in his seat and drapes his left wrist across the steering wheel. He holds the fingers on his right hand straight and tight together as he waves it back and forth through the air between us.

"I make it climb." He raises his hand to the roof. "Then swoosh." His voice whines like one of his planes as he swoops his hand down. Then he laughs.

I smile. The last bit of sun peeks through the trees and lights his face. I make a picture of him like this in my mind so I'll always have it. Just in case.

Chapter 8

Today in the library I read this book about a girl who is "different." I don't know anyone like her, anyone who reads a lot and wants to be a writer. But I think, *I'm* like that girl. I almost laugh out loud. I just wish the girl were real and lived here in Lake Haven.

At our lockers Roxanne always says hi. She wears a lot of black. Black T-shirts and fingernail polish.

"Hey," I ask. "Do you know anything about the school newspaper?"

"No, but my cousin works on it. She's totally in love with it. I hate school. I won't do anything that makes me stay later than I have to."

"Oh."

That night Dad sits with his head bent over his plate. He's quiet, but his eyes are soft and that vein in his neck isn't pulsing. He takes off his glasses and rubs his eyes.

"How was everyone's day?" Mom asks. Abby shrugs. Teddy won't look up.

"I aced my test," I say. "There was a question about

Paul Revere's ride. Next time I visit Boston, Aunt Jane said she'd take me to Bunker Hill."

"Who said you're going to Boston again?" Dad says. We look at him.

"Aunt Jane said I could." I hold the bottom of my chair with both hands.

"If *Aunt Jane* said so, then it must be true. What, so she's the boss now?"

I feel tears in my eyes but I use all my might to hold them back. "But you said if I got straight As then I could go. Uncle Terry and Aunt Jane—"

"Aunt Jane this, Aunt Jane that. You think you're so smart? Tell me what you're supposed to do when a sixty-inch casting has a crack down the middle of it!"

I grip the chair. If I want to go back next year, I must not say anything else, *ever,* about Aunt Jane and Boston. He glares at me.

"Huh? Miss Smarty Pants?"

Usually when he's like this I think about something else. Okay. Don't let him get to you. "I don't know."

He sits back in his chair and shoves his plate away. No one eats. Time has stopped.

I trudge up the stairs after dinner, Abby right behind me. I crawl under my bed and stare up at the box spring. There must be hundreds of tiny springs, all bunched together. I imagine them as a family, living and working together in perfect harmony.

"Want to go to Teddy's room?" Abby sits next to the bed. "Want to color?"

"No. I want some time to myself."

21

Two months ago today I was in Boston. Aunt Jane and Uncle Terry took me to restaurants, museums, and Nantucket. It was awesome. But I have to be careful. I can't set Dad off. Mom says this is the longest he's gone without drinking since he started in so heavily four years ago. If we keep things peaceful, he might quit for good.

Later Mom lies on my bed and sticks her head under to look at me. She hands me two Oreos. Her hair falls on the floor. Her chin is sharp and pointy as it faces the ceiling.

"We need to help him," she says. I know. But all I think about is how strangely normal her face looks, even though it's upside down.

Chapter 9

When Mrs. Hollis leaves the room during English, two girls begin talking. One is in front and the other behind me, and they lean to the side to talk because I'm in the way.

When we first moved here, people stared at me. But it's been more than a month and hardly anyone sees me anymore. At my old schools I always found someone to talk to. Here, it seems as if everybody has known each other forever and they already have a set of friends. Are all middle schools like this?

I start coughing, deep and hard. They stop and look at me.

"Go to the nurse," one girl says.

"I've already been to the nurse and about twenty doctors."

"What's the matter with you?" the other girl asks, her voice snotty.

"I caught malaria in India last summer. I was so sick I almost died. They had to airlift me to California. It was really traumatic. I almost died again."

"Of malaria?" the blond one asks.

"No, the plane crash-landed. The landing gear was broken."

Their eyes grow wide as they stare at me. Then Mrs. Hollis returns. They're bound to talk to me after class. I know I would. But when the bell rings, they walk away as if I'm not even there.

I wish I didn't care so much about having a friend.

Chapter 10

It's Friday and we're in the living room watching TV, but I'm watching Teddy. He's cute, even if he's my brother. He's short, with blue eyes, and with long brown hair like me. He has a gap between his two front teeth and a huge smile. It's been a long time since I've seen him smile.

He was happy when he played baseball with Pete and Harris in the lot near our old house. Last night he said, "I'm not going to make any friends here because we'll probably move." I put my hands over my ears and kept reading my history book.

Teddy stands and goes to the basement door again. He leans his head against the closed door and listens. "He's still screwing around with the engines."

We hear the faint whine of the plane engines. Teddy glances at me. I try to smile. We checked the basement yesterday, and we didn't find any bottles.

I wrap my blanket around my feet. I can't seem to get them warm. The bathroom window at school is *always* open. By the time lunch is over, I'm freezing.

I wonder if the reason Teddy usually makes friends so easily is because he knows what to say and do. I can't seem to figure that out. So I watch.

Today in the lunch line I watched that girl who talked to me in the bathroom the first day. Her name is Grace Bennett. She hangs out with the popular kids, but she talks to everybody.

Today she talked to this guy who nobody talks to. He drags his foot and wears goofy black glasses. All day I thought about this. Maybe it would make a good short story, and I have to write one for English. How this popular girl falls in love with him and her love is so strong that one day he wakes and the clubfoot is gone.

Now the doorbell rings. The engines stop whining, and Mom bolts off the couch.

She opens the front door only enough for her head to fit through. Abby and Teddy crowd behind her. I go to the window. Two women stand on the stoop, smiling. One holds a white basket in her hand.

"Welcome to Lake Haven," one woman says. "We're the Welcome Wagon. We've brought you all sorts of goodies from our wonderful community. Can we come in?"

Mom's back stiffens. Abby moves away from the door and takes my hand.

"We don't really need anything, but thank you." Mom begins to close the door.

"Wait, this won't take long." The other woman holds up the basket. I see tissue paper, a phone book, a hammer, and a box of chocolate. My mouth waters.

"That's nice, but we're fine." Mom closes the door so that it's only open a few inches. The women glance at each other. I look back at the basement door.

"Oh, dear, we should have called first," the first woman

says. "We'll leave this here for you. If you need anything, our numbers are in the basket. Again, welcome."

The women leave the basket on the stoop. I watch them turn and look at the house one last time before they get into their car. When it disappears around the corner, Teddy brings in the basket. We peek inside. There's also a coupon for Lake Haven Dry Cleaners, a candle, a golf tee, and a refrigerator magnet that says BOB'S LIQUORS.

When the plane engines start up again, we smile and I feel something warm trickle through my arms. I really wanted this basket.

Teddy clears his throat and holds up the basket. "Hi! She's welcome, and I'm the wagon. Or maybe I'm welcome and she's the wagon." He sounds just like the woman. He smiles and sticks his tongue through the gap in his teeth. We try not to laugh too hard.

Teddy gives me the chocolates, and I open the box and hand them around.

Chapter 11

I have my routine. I balance my sandwich on my lap and my milk on the toilet paper. I hold my book with my left hand. I make sure I'm done eating five minutes before the bell rings because that's when the groups pile in. I make sure my trash is stashed away in case someone knocks on my stall door. But no one ever does.

Today I wrap my legs around the toilet when I hear the door creak open.

"Meg?" It's Mrs. Fields, my social studies teacher. "Are you okay?"

"Yeah," I say.

"I saw you come in here twenty minutes ago. Come on out."

I'm about to tell her the malaria story and that I can't be away from a bathroom when I eat. But then I picture the way her lips pucker disapprovingly. She's the type to ask for a doctor's note.

I follow her into the lunchroom.

Where will I sit? Will they all laugh at me? Should I sit alone?

I see Roxanne and the hooded-sweatshirt girl I

noticed in the lunchroom on the first day. Roxanne smiles at me, and I slide into a seat next to her.

"This is Ariel, my cousin."

"Hi," I say. Ariel just stares at me.

I glance around and see Grace Bennett. What makes her so popular? Is it because she's friendly to everyone? But that doesn't make sense, because lots of popular kids never talk to anyone except other popular kids. I turn back to the table.

"Want an Oreo?" Roxanne hands me a plastic bag with a dozen Oreos in it.

I take one and twist it apart like I always do. I can't help grinning at her.

Chapter 12

If you want to be a writer, you have to read and write a lot. That's what Aunt Jane said when we were wandering around a bookstore in Boston. I'd never seen so many books. Books about architecture, food, religion. Books about other books. Books stacked to the ceiling and covering window seats.

She bought me four books she thought I'd like. But the best thing she bought me was a sketchbook. It's black and hardbacked, with 250 blank white pages. I could have gotten one with lines, but I like flipping through the empty pages.

"You should write in this as often as you can," she said. "Poems, stories, ideas. Jot down conversations you overhear."

I carry it with me wherever I go. I try to write in it a lot, but most of the time I don't know what to say. When I do write, I make sure my handwriting is small so I don't take up too much space. I don't want to fill it up and then not have it anymore.

Chapter 13

Dad works late tonight, so we have grilled cheeses for dinner. When he's home, we have to have real food, meat and potatoes and things like that.

The kitchen is a cinch to clean up, and it's still early.

"Let's go bowling." Mom claps her hands. "Let's celebrate."

"Celebrate what?" I ask as we put on our coats and go out into the night. The air is freezing and there's a full moon. Teddy calls shotgun and gets in the front seat.

"I might have a job," Mom says. "I interviewed for a part-time receptionist in a doctor's office. I think it went pretty good."

Abby smiles at me. I know what she's thinking. When Mom worked in a doctor's office two years ago, she had extra money to spend on us.

"But you don't know for sure if you have the job," Teddy says.

"Well, yeah, but I might have it and that's reason enough."

"Does Dad know about this?" Teddy folds his arms across his chest.

She starts the car. "No sense telling him until things are final."

"He won't like it."

"I can't think about that right now." Mom shakes her hair out of her eyes.

Don't you have enough to do around here? That's what Dad said when she told him about that job two years ago. But she did it anyway.

I watch how she grips the steering wheel with both hands and sits up straight, her shoulders pulled back. Her eyes dart from the road to the rearview mirror to the side mirror and back again to the road. She drives the speed limit.

At the bowling alley Mom shows us how far apart the fingers and thumb need to be on the ball. Even Teddy listens, because Mom is a great bowler. Before Mom's dad got sick when she was a kid, he took her bowling every weekend. Mom is so good that she's bowled a perfect game a whole bunch of times. She was the star on her league team all through high school.

"My dad used to bowl with his eyes closed." Mom takes off her shoes.

"Was that before or after he was sick?" Abby asks.

"Before."

"That's when you fed him and cut his toenails." Abby wrinkles her nose. I used to cringe, too, when Mom told these stories. But I don't want to be like that anymore.

Mom laughs. "When life gives you lemons, you make lemonade."

32

"When life gives you eggs, you make egg salad." I giggle.

"When life gives you pizza, you make . . ." Abby hesitates. "Ice cream."

"What?" Teddy and I say together. Then we laugh.

"Okay, sillies." Mom motions us up to the lane. "Bowling is one part skill, one part attitude. Bend your knees, stay low. But most important, when you let go you have to believe that the ball will give you a strike. Expect a strike. Think positive. That's attitude."

Mom takes her ball. "Okay, back up." She walks forward slowly, increases her speed, takes the ball back, bends her knee. And when she brings her arm down and lets go, the ball flies out of her hand as if it's come from a shotgun. *Strike.*

If I ever join a bowling league, I won't need anyone else on my team but Mom.

Chapter 14

Two days later we're in the kitchen playing cards when Dad walks in.

"Oh, Bob, now what have you gone and done?" Mom asks.

He's drunk.

"What?"

"You *know* what."

The cards are new and stiff, and the sound of Teddy's shuffling fills the room. For a moment I hear the cards saying, *No! Nonononononononononono!*

"Stop it," Dad says. When Teddy won't, Dad grabs at the cards. They spill onto the floor. Teddy stands and throws his chair against the table. "Pick them up," Dad demands.

"No!" Teddy says.

"I'll help, Teddy," I say. Why doesn't he let things be, the way we've always done?

"No, he did it! He grabbed the cards. *You* pick them up." Teddy points at Dad.

Abby presses next to me. I put my arms around her. I feel as if I'm holding my breath.

"Stop, both of you." Mom leans down and begins picking up the cards.

"He should do it, Ma," Teddy yells.

"I'll have it done in a second," Mom says.

"He should do it!" Teddy screams.

"There." She puts the cards on the table.

"You disrespectful runt," Dad says. "You crybaby."

Teddy starts toward Dad, but Mom jumps between them. She holds Teddy by the shoulders. His face is twisted and red, and wet with tears. I feel paralyzed. Abby screams in my ear but it sounds far away, as if it's coming from the next room.

"That's it," Mom says. "Get your coats, kids."

Out on the highway Mom lets the car fly, as if we're never going back.

We sit in a booth in McDonald's. The lights are bright and the room is freezing.

"Six months," Mom says. "He went six months."

"This is going to be like last time," Teddy says.

"I can't believe that. When you were little, he went years without . . ." Mom shakes her head. "You both have such tempers."

"He started it." Teddy finishes putting the jacket and boots on Abby's Polly Pocket doll and hands it back to her.

"You know he says things he doesn't mean," Mom says.

Teddy shrugs. "He doesn't bother me."

"When I first met him, you should have seen him. . . ." Mom's voice trails off.

"You mean when you took him to get that haircut?" Abby scoops the last of her sundae into her mouth.

On their first date Mom took Dad to get his long hair cut and to buy new jeans. She cleaned him up, that was what everyone said to her at the plant where they worked.

"Oh, he made everyone laugh. You know how he is."

But I frown. "Yeah, well, he's not so funny tonight."

Tears spring to Mom's eyes. Dad is a big fat liar. Before we moved, he said, I'm going to stop drinking. He promised. And now Mom's crying. I wish we'd gone bowling.

"If only we could get him to AA," Mom says. "He won't listen to me."

"Maybe he'd listen to somebody else," I say without thinking. Teddy and Mom whip their heads to look at me. Abby stops playing with her Polly Pocket.

"And just who do you think we'd get to help us?" Mom asks.

I shrug and sink in my seat.

"We don't know anyone here," Mom says. "Besides, you know where all that can lead. This is our business."

Teddy's cheeks redden as he spins his empty sundae cup on the table. Three years ago Teddy let it slip to Uncle Terry that Dad was drinking. After Uncle Terry talked to him about it, Dad was so angry that he wouldn't speak to Teddy for months.

Teddy stares at my uneaten sundae. I push it across the table so it's in front of him. He doesn't exactly smile, but his brows rise as he plunges his spoon into the chocolate.

Chapter 15

Ariel and Roxanne are cousins, twice removed, through their mothers. Ariel has red hair and braces and better than perfect eyesight. Roxanne tells me they communicate with each other by sending brain waves.

I sit with them every day. Roxanne likes to point out people, and Ariel gives thumbs up or down. Jennifer Conway gets two thumbs down because she's stuck-up and hates Roxanne. Hannah Solmas gets two thumbs down because she once laughed at Ariel's cartwheel in gym class. One day when Roxanne points to Grace Bennett, Ariel sticks her thumb down.

"You *have* to give Grace Bennett the thumbs-up," Roxanne says. "She brought you those books when you had your appendix out. She's, like, the school's nicest person."

Ariel sighs and flips her long red hair out of her face. "She's too nice."

"How can you be too nice?" I've never heard of such a thing.

Ariel shrugs. "No one is *that* perfect. Plus she hangs out with Jennifer's crowd. But I have to say that she's a very good artist, and I respect that. I respect her for her art."

Roxanne snorts and crosses her arms. Her black rubber bracelets slip down her arm. "Oh, that's ridiculous. Give her a break. She's had *such* a tragic life."

She turns to me. I lean forward. "Grace's mom died of cancer when Grace was in third grade. Then a couple of years later her dad married one of Grace's mom's friends. It was a big scandal."

I see Grace at the popular table, but she's not talking to anyone. She stares at something across the cafeteria, and I follow her eyes.

Maybe she's thinking about how much she misses her mom. I picture my mom and how her face fell when she found out she didn't get the job in the doctor's office. I bite the cuticle on my thumb. I don't want anything bad to happen to Mom.

Chapter 16

This is what Mrs. Hollis wrote on my short story: *Good writing and a great imagination! The sympathy the girl has for the boy with the clubfoot is very real. I'd love to see you write something else that's not fantasy based but that comes from your life.*

I don't *want* to write about my life. Who cares about that? Why would I ever want to tell anyone what's going on at home? And I don't think it's such a big fantasy that a girl's love could cure a boy's clubfoot.

Well, maybe it is.

Maybe I could write that he doesn't want to do anything about his clubfoot because he knows it would really hurt. But her love encourages him to get an operation.

I'm not a quitter. I like getting good grades. Two years ago at an assembly, my teacher, Miss Hemphill, gave me a certificate for being the fourth grader with the best grades. I stood on the stage while everyone clapped. It was the greatest feeling I've ever had.

"You should join the school newspaper," Mrs. Hollis says to me after class. "There's a meeting tomorrow."

How could she have known I've been thinking about that for the past month?

"You're a good writer," she says. "The newspaper needs you."

This is so cool. I tell Aunt Jane all about it when she calls after dinner.

"I'm so proud of you," she says. I smile and puff out my chest.

Then I go upstairs and sit at my desk and open my sketchbook. I roll my pencil between my finger and thumb. Now it's just my story and me, and that feels good.

Two days later Mrs. Hollis stops me in the hall. She's tall and thin, and when she's not wearing her glasses they hang from a chain around her neck. "Why didn't you come to the newspaper meeting?"

I'd walked up to the room the day before and had seen it full of girls and a few boys laughing, joking. I didn't see Ariel. One girl looked at me, and I swear she started laughing. I backed out and ran the other way.

"I had to help my little sister. I can't go to after-school meetings because she has these ulcer attacks and I never know when I'll have to go meet her and walk her home."

"Ulcer attacks?" Mrs. Hollis asks. "She's so young." Then her eyes get soft, as if she's about to cry. And I like it when she puts her arm around me.

"You just never know when she's going to have one."

"Let me know how I can help." Squeeze.

I don't want her to ask me any more questions, so I

look around the hall. Grace Bennett smiles as she walks by. Mrs. Hollis calls her over.

"Meg is interested in the newspaper. She's a writer. Grace is our staff artist."

"Great!" Grace starts telling me about the paper as Mrs. Hollis walks away. I hold my books to my chest and watch her lips move. Her teeth are whiter than any I've ever seen. I think about her mom dying and wonder if she ever dreams about her. Then she sees my sketchbook.

"What? You have one of these, too?" She grabs my sketchbook. With her other hand she reaches into her backpack and pulls out a sketchbook, identical to mine. She holds them both in the air. "I don't know anyone else who has one of these!"

"My aunt bought it for me in Boston."

"I got mine in Chicago." She shows me some of her pages, which are filled with colors and smudges and drawings of people. Some pages are so bright and busy that I feel as if I need to step back to see everything.

She closes her book and looks at me. "What do you have in yours?"

"Oh, I can't draw. I just write in mine."

"What do you like to write?" Her eyes are blue, like the sky, and when she smiles her lips are kind of crooked. I suddenly feel as if I can tell her anything.

"Stories," I blurt out.

"It's *so* great to meet someone who likes this kind of thing." She lowers her voice and touches my shoulder. "I get sick of talking about sports and stuff, don't you?"

I nod. I've never met anyone who is excited about the

same things as me. If Grace works for the newspaper, then maybe I can do it, too.

"I know!" she says. "You write books, and I'll draw the pictures. Then we'll move to New York and be business partners and be famous!"

For the life of me I can't understand why Ariel thinks it's bad to be so nice.

The next day in the lunch line Grace asks, "Have you started writing?" She doesn't wait for my answer. "How about you write a mystery about these two girls who solve crimes, and I'll draw the pictures."

We hurry to a table.

"Maybe the girls can talk to each other using brain waves," I say. "And maybe they live on an island, like Nantucket. Have you ever been there?"

"No, but I'd like to," Grace says.

"I bet I can get you some pictures so you'll know what to draw."

"Yeah, okay."

I open my milk. "I think the girls should investigate robberies, not murders."

"Yeah, and they give their reward money to charities," Grace says.

"And they're best friends."

"And they live next door to each other."

"And they tell each other everything."

"You should come to my house tomorrow so we can start," Grace says.

The bell rings. I've been talking so much that I'm dizzy when I look around the lunchroom. I see Roxanne and Ariel at our table. I smile, but Ariel turns away and I don't know if she's seen me or not. I look down at my tray. I barely ate. Grace's tray is still full, too.

In art I laugh at my mistakes. I raise my hand in history more than usual. I miss the bus so I can walk home and think about my story. It's cold and windy, but I don't care. It will be more than a story. It'll be a book. With lots of details, clues, and false leads. Maybe I'll use the inn where Aunt Jane and I had lunch.

I'm so full of ideas and things to say!

Then I see Dad's truck in the driveway and remember that he's working an early shift. Numbness seeps up my legs. The house looks quiet. So is the inside of my head.

"Where have you been?" Abby waits for me by the front door until I'm inside.

"I missed the bus."

"Dad's in the basement."

Mom tries to smile. I'm suddenly so sleepy that I want to take a nap. Abby follows me upstairs. Teddy's door is shut but I hear music from inside.

I sit, open my sketchbook, and stare at the wall. Then I picture how one side of Grace's lip is crooked when she smiles. A tingle races up my back, and I start to write.

Chapter 17

Grace lives in a big old house near town. The bookcase in the living room stretches to the ceiling, and it's filled with books. She has her own bedroom *and* bathroom. They even have two staircases.

The only other time I've been in a house like this was when we lived in Ohio. Mary Rose Griffin and I sat together every day on the bus. A couple of times I went home with her, and we played hide-and-seek in the third-floor rooms. But then we moved to Michigan, and I never saw her again.

Grace's room is a mess, with colored pencils and papers all over the place. We shove the papers aside and sit on her bed and talk about our book. I make notes in my sketchbook. We decide that the girls are named Samantha and Emily, and that they're in sixth grade. Grace wants the girls to have cool moms who are best friends, too.

After a while we go to the kitchen. Grace's stepmom sits with us.

Her fingers feel so strong when she shakes my hand. "Please call me Carollyn."

She's pretty and healthy-looking, with long hair that

she pulls back into a ponytail. I ask tons of questions. Carollyn tells me that she grew up here and that she's a nurse who delivers babies. She doesn't even care that we eat the whole bowl of grapes.

Carollyn isn't what I imagined from the story Roxanne told me about her. She's the kind of person who turns her body toward you when she talks, as if you're the most important person in the world. I like that. I wonder if what Roxanne told me is even true.

It's dark when we get into Carollyn's car. The sky is spitting snowflakes, and I watch as they fall on the windshield and melt. The closer we get to my house, the sadder I am. How great would it be to live at Grace's house!

"Here Grace and I've been talking our heads off and we've barely asked you any questions," Carollyn says. "How do you like Lake Haven?"

I see Dad's truck in our driveway. Our house looks small and dingy. We don't have any bookcases or fireplaces or winding staircases. Grace said her dad is a dentist. And a runner.

"I like it." What if they ask to come inside? When Carollyn stops the car, I open the door.

"Wait," she says. "Maybe we can come in and meet your folks."

"Oh, no. My mom has this awful stomach flu. She threw up all last night."

"Oh, my, I'm sorry," Carollyn says.

I hold on to the outside of the car door. The metal feels cold and sharp. I don't know what to do. This morning at breakfast, Teddy and Abby stared at me as I ate.

"What will you say if Grace asks about Dad?" Teddy asked.

"What's there to tell?" I shrugged. Teddy nodded, and so did Abby.

Now Grace smiles at me.

"Maybe the girls meet this famous old lady, a writer, who is staying at the inn, and someone robs her," I say.

"Yeah, and I could make her look really cool with silver hair and pearls, and maybe she's tall," Grace says.

"The lady is so impressed with them that she hires them to find her stolen jewels."

"And maybe the robbers hide the jewels in a cave. I'm good at drawing caves."

"What are you girls talking about?" Carollyn asks.

"We're writing a book," Grace says. There's something thrilling about the sound of this. We giggle, and I feel as if we're the last two people left in the world.

Chapter 18

Pricilla Principal stands on the veranda and looks out over the shimmering ocean. She's stately-looking and hugely famous and hugely nice. But she's crying. Emily walks up to the famous author with her latest book in her hand.

"What's the matter?" Emily asks.

"Someone has stolen my jewelry," Pricilla says.

"I think I can help you," Emily says. As she stands there looking at Pricilla, she sends Samantha brain waves. "Come and meet me. We have another case to solve."

Chapter 19

On Thanksgiving, Dad sits in his chair and taps his hand on the end table until I think I'm going crazy. Thump. Thump. Thump. He flips through the TV stations.

"You got to be kidding me, who would ever want to buy that crap?" he barks at a commercial. Flip, flip, flip. Thump, thump, thump. "Abby, get me coffee!"

When we were little, Teddy made Pilgrim hats out of newspaper, and Abby and I decorated them and wore them during dinner. Today we silently peel potatoes, play cards, and wait.

When we finally sit down for dinner, Dad is calmer. It's as if his anxiety has exhausted him. That's when I start feeling angry. This is Thanksgiving! We should be happy and celebrating. He ruins everything.

Grace told me that Carollyn cooks for twenty-five people, and that's not even all her relatives. Uncle Terry and Aunt Jane call. They're with friends in New York. I imagine how nice it would be to feel relaxed and happy while you're having turkey dinner.

Two nights later Grace and I lie side by side in sleeping bags on the floor in her room. I packed and unpacked three times before deciding what to bring. Slippers? A robe? Real pajamas or sweats? To be on the safe side, I bring everything, and now I'm wearing sweatpants because that's what Grace wears.

We had dinner in the dining room (with candles and place mats) with her dad, Jim, Carollyn, and her ten-year-old brother, Ricky. I didn't know what to do. My elbows were on the table, then off. We had Chinese food, and should I eat with chopsticks or a fork?

Grace's dad told us about a patient who had a disease and needed all his teeth pulled. It was so interesting. Then questions just came flying out of me. How do you get this disease? How do you pull teeth? What do you do with the blood? How do you know how much Novocain to give?

After that he asked *me* questions—What do you like to do? Who is your favorite writer? Questions that were fun to answer.

Now, in the dark, I look at Grace. The night-light shines on her face. We planned to talk about our book tonight, but I ask, "So, did your dad grow up here, too?"

"No, North Carolina. He moved here when he married my mom." Her voice lingers over the word *mom*.

"When did she die?"

"When I was eight. She had breast cancer." Then she tells me this terrible story. Her mom had all these operations and treatments. Everyone told Grace that her mom

49

would pull through. "They said the radiation was *working*. That's what everyone *said*."

Grace squeezes her eyes shut so tight that the lines in her skin run all the way to her jaw. Then she relaxes her face and opens her eyes.

"She just got sicker and sicker. One day she said, 'You have to be strong. I want your dad to be happy. You and Ricky will need a mom. That's okay. I want that.' So my mom introduced us to Carollyn, who was a friend of hers from high school. And there you go."

I look at the ceiling. You'd think Grace's mom wouldn't want anyone to take her place. But she was taking care of her kids. I've never heard of such a thing.

Grace starts to cry. When Teddy cries, he runs away. But I have this feeling Grace wants to talk. I ask her: Where were you when your mom died? Do you dream about her? What did she look like? She answers and doesn't seem to care that I hear her crying.

I think Grace is the bravest person I've ever met.

In the morning we roll up our sleeping bags, and I wonder if Grace is embarrassed by everything she told me. But she smiles and looks me in the eyes. She trusts me.

We stop at a diner for breakfast on our way to my house. We sit in a booth, and I see our reflection in the window: one happy family. I don't have a single worry.

Then Carollyn asks, "Why did you and your family move here?"

"My dad runs the foundry." I hadn't planned to say this, but it slips out.

"Towdan Casting? I thought John McDonald runs it. Is he no longer there?"

My cheeks burn. "I don't mean that he runs the *whole* foundry. Just a *section*."

They look at me. Dr. Bennett has wrinkly lines across his forehead, and Carollyn stops her fork just before putting it into her mouth. I want to crawl under the table and stay there for the rest of my life. Why did I say that? They know I'm not telling the truth.

I cut my pancakes into teeny pieces. It hurts to look at them.

Then Dr. Bennett says, "How about a game of Whaddya Think?" He points to a man, woman, boy, and girl who stand at the checkout counter. Grace tells me how to play. You have to come up with a story about what that family is doing. Best story wins.

Ricky goes first. "The boy is begging them for another candy bar."

"They just looked at a new house, and the boy doesn't want to move, and they're telling him how great the new house will be because it has a pool," Dr. Bennett says.

I burst in before Grace or Carollyn can say anything.

"They've returned from a camping trip in Australia, where they found this little boy. When he was a teeny baby, smugglers kidnapped him and left him in the outback after his real family couldn't pay the ransom. Then a family of wild kangaroos raised him in the woods until *this* family found him and adopted him. He doesn't understand English and they're taking him all around town and explaining things. Every so often his new sister hops up and down like a kangaroo to make him feel at home."

I stare at the people while I talk. When I finish, I turn back to our table. Everyone has funny looks on their faces. Did I do something wrong again? Then Dr. Bennett laughs and says, "You win! That's some story."

I smile. Maybe they forgot what I said about the foundry.

Chapter 20

Jennifer Conway hurries into the newspaper room, darting her eyes around and snapping her gum. She throws herself into a chair, yanking on her long brown ponytail.

"I want you to know, I don't have a lot of time," she says to no one in particular.

She won't look at anyone except Grace. When Grace smiles, Jennifer rolls her eyes at all of us. But Grace just keeps smiling. How can anyone as snotty as Jennifer get elected sixth-grade class president?

Ariel and I watch from the back of the classroom. Ariel throws her notebook on a desk and turns to Mrs. Hollis. "Look at her. I'm not going to interview her. I *won't.*"

"Well, somebody has to," Mrs. Hollis says, chuckling. They look at me.

"Okay." I have no idea what I'm supposed to do. Why did I say okay? But this is my first newspaper meeting, and I'm afraid to ask. I walk slowly to the front of the room.

Jennifer wears a soft pink sweater. Expensive. She looks like lots of girls at the schools I've attended. Pretty.

Popular. But I never talked to any of them. Grace waves to me from the drafting table, and I smile back.

I sit next to Jennifer, thinking of the interview the paper did with the seventh-grade president last week. I'll borrow questions from that. My heartbeat quickens. I clear my throat. Jennifer looks at me.

"So." I try to swallow. Jennifer flutters her eyes and cracks her gum again. Her legs bounce under the desk. I feel my heartbeat slow down. "Let's go over there, by the door, so we can talk."

We push two desks together and sit down. No one can hear us now. "Okay. What kind of mark do you want to leave on the sixth grade this year?"

Jennifer stops chewing. "*Mark?* What? Look, I don't want to sound stupid."

I put my pencil down. How could I possibly make someone like her sound stupid?

"I mean, who are you, anyway?"

"I'm Meg. I moved here over the summer." She chews her gum and looks around. I frown and lower my voice. "I've been around newspapers my whole life. My grandpa practically started the *Chicago Tribune*. I know how to write."

She stops chewing and wrinkles her nose. I stare right at her.

"Okay, well. Wow. I didn't mean to . . . I didn't want . . . Oh, I don't know what to do." She really looks at me for the first time. Her eyes are the most unusual color, gray or yellow or maybe even gold. I feel almost hypnotized as I watch them grow bigger.

She doesn't say anything else and then looks down at her fingers. Some of her nails are painted green, while others are blue. I look at her eyes again. She's really pretty. And I can tell she doesn't want to be president.

"Well," I say. "Maybe you could talk about how you got elected president."

"Our volleyball team played Michigan City—you know, our big rival—and I served all those aces and that reporter wrote about it in the newspaper. Everybody read it, and then someone said, run for class president, everyone knows you! What am I going to do now? I don't know anything about being president."

I'm so surprised that I sit back in my seat. I don't know anything about being president, either, but I remember the interview I read.

"You should talk about hosting a dance and how you hope our class raises enough money to buy a nice gift for the school. And that we have more school spirit than the seventh or eighth graders. And maybe you should thank everyone for voting for you."

Jennifer nods. "Yeah, yeah. Say all that. And make me look good, okay? *Please?*"

She stands and pushes the desk back into place. I guess the interview is over. Marty Nicklas takes her picture. Not once does Jennifer look at me. Not even when she tells everyone goodbye and leaves.

Later, as Grace and I wait for our rides home, I ask, "Are you friends with Jennifer?"

"Oh, yeah. I've known her since preschool."

I nod. "Jennifer is kind of . . . well . . . bossy."

Grace stares out the window. "But she can be nice."

I look out the window, too. Maybe I just didn't see Jennifer's nice side. Maybe nothing is wrong with her. Maybe something is wrong with me.

Chapter 21

Aunt Jane calls to say that she and Uncle Terry are coming after Christmas. I stand at the window and watch a moving van pull up to the house across the street. I talk so much my throat hurts: Grace, my As in school, our book. I tell Aunt Jane about my Great Faces project in history. We have to research and write a report about a famous person.

"What about a woman, like Eleanor Roosevelt?" she asks. "She was fascinating."

"Okay. I'll look up some stuff about her." What else can I say to keep her talking?

"How are things at home?" she asks, her voice softer, slower.

"Good." I walk into the kitchen, where Teddy is reading. "I have to go now. Bye."

I hang up and glance at Teddy. "Someone is moving in across the street." He stares at me. But I've done nothing wrong. I've told Aunt Jane nothing about Dad.

Most days Grace is already sitting with her friends by the time I get to the lunchroom. The past couple of days she came to my table just before lunch ended. Today she waits for me, and we go through the line together. Then we walk into the lunchroom. Off to my right I see the table with Grace's friends. Roxanne and Ariel sit in our usual spot. Ariel watches me, lips pinched.

I don't want Ariel and Roxanne mad at me because I want to sit with Grace. So I don't move. When I look at Grace, she smiles and we laugh. She hasn't moved, either.

"Come on, we'll go over here," Grace says finally. I follow her to my table. Ariel scoots over to let Grace sit next to her, but she won't look at her.

"Hi, Ariel. Hi, Roxanne." Grace beams at them. Ariel still won't look at her.

"So, Grace, Ariel heard something that *your friend* Hannah said," Roxanne says.

I don't like the way she said *your friend*, but Grace looks interested. "What?"

"She heard Hannah say that Meg caught malaria last summer. But get this. She couldn't remember if Meg caught it in South America or at the South Pole."

Ariel points to Hannah across the lunchroom. I turn to look. She's tall, with frizzy blond hair and braces. When I turn back, Grace is looking at me, her head tilted. I want to slide off my chair. How will I explain this?

Roxanne and Ariel look at each other and roll their eyes.

"She's even dumber than we imagined," Roxanne says. "Did you tell her that malaria comes from mosquitoes and there aren't any at the South Pole?"

Ariel laughs as if she's never heard anything so funny. She keeps telling stories about the dumb things Hannah has said since first grade. I suck in my breath, praying they won't ask me about this. Then the bell rings.

Later Grace says, "That's so weird that Hannah said you had malaria."

She waits, as if she wants me to explain. I feel hot, and my mouth goes dry. Then I roll my eyes and laugh. "I can't miss my bus!" And I run down the hall.

Chapter 22

Mom sips her coffee. We're in the restaurant at the front of the bowling alley. She's been crying. When we hear cheers, Mom raises her eyebrows and turns toward the lanes.

"Somebody is having a good game." She smiles faintly.

"Can't we play?" Abby asks for the tenth time.

"Not tonight." Mom pulls her hair off her forehead.

I sit up. "How did your dad get so good at bowling?" I already know the story. I just want to hear it again. Teddy spins the glass ashtray on the table.

"He had a job at a bowling alley when he was a boy. At that time the lanes had to have people, not machines, set the pins. So that was his job. Then he played."

"Tell the story about when all those people came in at once," Abby says.

"We've already heard that." Teddy keeps glancing at the door.

"There was a party, and the other boy who set the pins didn't show up. Dad had to set all six lanes himself. He did such a good job that one of the men gave him a twenty-dollar tip. Back then that bought groceries for a week."

She's smiling now, and I sit back in my seat.

"How come your mom didn't ever go bowling?" Abby asks.

"She didn't like it," Mom says. "She didn't like much of anything, really."

"Did she have a job?" I ask. Our grandmother lives in Michigan. Mom says she's too old to travel. I don't know why we never go there.

"No, she stayed home. Then when my dad got sick, she had to take care of him."

"So how come *she* didn't cut his toenails?" Abby scrunches her nose.

Mom stares at her coffee cup.

"I don't see what this has to do with Dad," Teddy says. We all look at him. "I don't see why we have to leave the house all the time."

"I don't trust you two anymore when he's drinking," Mom says.

"But we always leave now, and what if someone comes to the door and we're not there? Or what if he goes in the yard or something? What if the neighbors are outside?"

"It's too dark, too cold," Mom says. "No one is outside. And he won't leave."

"You don't know that." Teddy crosses his arms and sinks in his seat.

Mom's right. It's dark. No way will kids be playing kickball in front of our house tonight. We don't have to worry, not like the time in Michigan when Dad demanded a turn in our game, kicked and missed, and then fell on his face. The neighbor kids laughed and then told the story every time we played kickball after that.

But he *could* go into the garage, and someone *might* see him. Maybe we should go home. Do something.

When I look around, I see a man in a booth, cradling a cup of coffee in his hands. He wears a black coat and hat, and he seems nervous. Is he a spy, here to meet his contact? Did he leave a bag of money in the bathroom and he's waiting for instructions about what to do next? I saw a movie about that once.

Maybe this is what one of the jewelry thieves in our book looks like. Emily sees him in a coffee shop and has this bad feeling about him. She follows him and discovers the cave. She finds the jewels just as the other robbers come back.

For a moment I'm transported into that cave, and I feel the coolness of the rocks against my fingertips. The fear as the robbers surprise me from behind.

I want to disappear into a corner and write. I have so much to say about this story.

We turn when we hear more cheers. Mom sits up, lifting her face. "Someone just threw a strike."

Chapter 23

When I get into bed tonight, Abby jumps out of hers and in with me. "What's Grace's house like?"

"I don't know. Regular."

"Does she have a sister?"

"Just a brother. He's ten."

"Are you going to sleep over there again?"

"I don't know."

"What do you do over there?"

"We talk and write and draw. Grace is a really good artist."

"Like me!"

Abby puts her feet against my shin, and they're so cold that my heart skips a beat. But I let her feet stay there until I hear her breathing deeply. Then I get up, get into her bed, and stare at the ceiling. Today Grace said to me, "When can I come over to your house?"

"As soon as everyone is better. Abby has that stomach thing now."

She tilted her head and looked at me. "How old is Abby?"

"Seven."

"Does Teddy have it, too?"

"He did, but now he's better."

Grace lowered her head and spun her fork on the table. She looked so disappointed. I didn't want to keep telling her stories, but I didn't know what else to do.

"They can't wait to meet you," I said. "I talk about you all the time. My mom said, 'As soon as I'm better, we'll have Grace over.'"

She brightened. "Did you tell them about our book?"

I nodded, though it wasn't true. All we seem to talk about is Dad.

"I want to show it to Carollyn and my dad. You have such a cool imagination."

Now I smile in the dark. Then I turn over and stare at the wall.

Chapter 24

On Saturday the smell of bacon and eggs wakes me. The radio in the kitchen is playing an oldies station, and Dad hums as he stands over the stove.

"Rise and shine, Meggie," he says. His back is to me, and for a second a creepy feeling runs through me. How does he know I'm standing here?

"Where is everyone?" Three presents, wrapped in newspaper, are on the table. But it's not anyone's birthday.

"Still sleeping! On a beautiful day like today. But not you and me."

Last year when he told us he was done drinking and we were moving to Lake Haven, he gave us all new CD players.

"Are we moving again?" I hold my breath.

"No! It's been a tough time. I want to make it up to you. I've stopped drinking."

"What about going to AA?" My voice is soft.

He looks at me over the top of his glasses. "People don't need to know our business. Besides, I know what those meetings are like. Old men sitting around telling their sad, pitiful stories. I hear enough pitiful stories at work. I just need help from the family."

He gives me a plate of eggs and toast with peanut butter, just the way I like it. He drums his fingers on the table. Those fingers are like little people, running in place.

I bite into my toast. Dad smiles; then he frowns when a new song comes on. "Crappy station."

He wakes everyone and they creep into the kitchen. Abby leans into my arm as she eyes the presents. Teddy drops into a chair and rubs his eyes. Mom pours herself a cup of coffee and stands with one hand on her hip. "What's all this?"

"Some things I thought you'd like. Abby, do you want scrambled or over easy?"

She leans into me harder and doesn't answer.

Mom sighs loudly. "Bob, we don't need presents. We need you to stop drinking."

"I know, I know. And I am. I'm done drinking. This is it."

"You said that last time," she says.

"I know. But things are different now."

"How are they different?" Mom asks.

"You'll see." He hands Abby a present. She waits for Mom to nod, and then she tears open the paper. She holds a doll with soft brown hair and eyes that open and close. My package is heavy, and when I open it I suck in my breath. It's a very expensive microscope with a book of science experiments.

I can see from the shape of Teddy's present that it's a skateboard. But when Dad hands it to him, Teddy says, "I don't need to be bribed."

"Oh, big man, think you know everything, huh?" Dad

says sharply. Teddy starts for the living room. "Bet you don't know about this one, big man."

He hands Mom an envelope. She opens it, pulls out a paper, and covers her mouth with her other hand as she stares.

Teddy looks around her shoulder. Dad turns up the radio and moves to the stove, humming again.

"What is it?" Abby asks.

"It's a check for three thousand dollars," Teddy says.

I push Abby away and go to Mom. I've never seen a check for that much money.

"I told you everything is different here," Dad says. "I saved the company a boatload of money when I figured out how to work with the crack in the casting. I got this as a bonus."

"Wow." Teddy fiddles with the newspaper that covers his present.

"We'll sit on this money for a while," Dad says. "Maybe we'll go on a vacation."

"Disney World!" Abby yells. All of us laugh.

Then Dad pretends that the spatula is a microphone and says, "And Mr. Higgins, what are you going to do now that you've won the jackpot?"

"I'm going to Disney World!"

I close my eyes. If I didn't know better, I'd think Mr. Higgins was right here. When I look up, Mom is standing next to Dad. She puts her head on his shoulder.

Teddy grins at me as I dive into my eggs. Maybe all Dad needed was encouragement and good news. Hope rushes at me like the wind.

Chapter 25

School is a lot more fun now that Grace and I are friends. People say hi to me all the time in the hallways. Sometimes I feel as if I'm in a dream. I've met more people here in three months than in the two years I spent at our last school. Grace knows everyone, and now they think I'm okay. People look at me instead of *through* me.

Today during homeroom we get the new issue of our newspaper. My interview with Jennifer is only four paragraphs long, but it's on the front page. I glance at her picture, but mostly I stare at my name. *By Meg Summers.* How cool is that?

After our newspaper meeting, Grace and I spread the paper across the drafting table. We think the editorial about school lunches is great. We laugh at Grace's cartoon. We think the football article is too long. Then we look at the front page again.

Ariel comes up behind us. "Listen to Jennifer. 'I think we'll have a great year and make lots of money to buy something special for the school in the spring.' You must be such a good writer, Meg, that you even make someone like *her* look good."

I stare so hard at the paper that my eyes blur. What if they find out that I made this up?

When Ariel walks away, Grace says, "That's nice. You know, everybody thinks she's one of the best editors on the paper."

I nod but don't look her in the eyes.

The next day I see Ariel coming toward me in the hall. I cut through the crowd until I'm in front of her, and then I say hello. I know she sees me, on account of her perfect eyesight. But she just keeps walking.

Does she know I made up the article on Jennifer? Maybe she's talking to Roxanne through brain waves. But then I get angry. We sit together at lunch. We work at the paper. Aren't we friends? Is she angry that I like Grace, too?

There are so many things about being friends that I don't understand.

Chapter 26

"You have to sleep over at Grace's house *again*?" Abby asks.

I stuff my sketchbook in my bag as Abby follows me down the stairs. Teddy is eating ice cream in the kitchen.

"What if Grace wants to come here?" Teddy asks.

I shrug. Then I think about how Teddy always raced out the door when he saw Pete and Harris coming down the street. Now I wonder. Did he tell tall tales about our family to his friends, too?

Grace's house looks like the inside of a magazine. There's a wreath on the front door and white lights on the bushes. An enormous tree stands in the corner near the fireplace. At breakfast on Sunday Carollyn heats something on the stove that smells like cinnamon and says, "After church we're making cookies."

I sit at the counter and line up the jars of sprinkles. They're taking me home after church, but if I were to stay I'd do a good job with these sprinkles.

Last night, after I explained how dark and mysterious the jewelry thieves are, Carollyn stared at me as if it was the most *interesting* thing she'd ever heard. When I finished she hugged me.

"I love your stories. No wonder you and Grace have such a good time together."

"Yeah, but Grace has lots of friends," I said.

"But not many of them have as much in common as you two do. You're special."

Even this morning that still makes me feel good.

"Do you have your Christmas tree up yet?" Carollyn asks.

Grace and Ricky are next to me. Someone on the stereo sings "White Christmas."

"Not yet." I push thoughts of my house out of my head.

Ricky stares at me, his milk mustache sparkling under the lights. He has blond hair, like Grace, and big blue eyes. "But Christmas is in two weeks!"

I stop eating. Is it wrong not to have a tree up yet? Then I think about a TV movie I once saw. "We wait because every year we go into the woods and cut down our own tree. If you do it too early the sap in the tree will harden and the needles will fall off."

I don't know what I'm talking about, but I keep going. "Then we make our own ornaments out of things like pop cans and tinfoil. On Christmas morning we bake doughnuts from a special recipe that's been passed down in our family for two hundred years."

"Wow, that's so cool," Ricky says.

I stare out the window as we ride to church. We've never cut down our own tree. Our decorations came from a gas station in Ohio that ran a sale on red and silver bulbs.

I don't want Ricky to ask me anything else, so I ask him tons of questions. How many LEGOs do you have? What happens if you lose a piece? Won't that mess up what you're building? I'm safe once we sit in church, but then through the whole service I shiver—it is *so* cold. Grace has the perfect family, and I lied to them. Again.

After church we help Carollyn serve coffee in Fellowship Hall. It's decorated with a Christmas tree and wreaths, and someone plays "Joy to the World" on a piano. This old lady with poufy blue hair and a cane comes up the line. She has a couple of cookies on her plate, and she asks Grace to help her to a chair and bring her coffee. After Grace says, "Sure," the lady looks at me and says, "Grace is such a dear. Such a happy girl."

Grace smiles, but when she turns I see that smile slide right off her face. Then she walks out the door. I find her in the pantry, staring at the empty shelves.

"Are you okay?"

"I'm just hanging on." She's crying softly.

Hanging on to what? I sit on a stool and stare at the empty shelves with her. "You're thinking about your mom, aren't you?"

She nods. "She used to make this awesome lemon cookie every Christmas. We begged her to make it during the year, but she wouldn't. It was special, only for Christmas, she used to say. It was the best thing I'd ever tasted."

"I'm sorry."

"She loved Christmas. I remember that. I do. That's one thing I really remember."

We stay like this for a few minutes. Then Grace sighs and we go back to our place behind the coffee table. She knows everyone, and soon she's smiling again. No one would ever know that she'd just been in the pantry crying.

In the car I wonder about Grace. She was pretending in church. Pretending to be happy so people wouldn't worry about her. Or ask what was wrong. She doesn't want anyone to know how she feels.

But why did it seem so easy for her to talk to me?

Dr. Bennett stops at my house. "Maybe we can meet your folks."

"Oh, no, my mom is just getting over the stomach flu."

"Again?" Carollyn turns to me.

I suck in my breath and nod, thank them a bunch, and shoot out the door.

Chapter 27

Eleanor Roosevelt was the wife of Franklin Delano Roosevelt, who was president during World War II. In a book I find a picture of her standing by a pond. She has on these old-looking shoes and a big bulky coat, and she holds a little purse under her arm.

She looks like a grandma. We never see my mom's mom, and I never knew Dad's mom. Did they ever dress like this? With my finger I trace Eleanor Roosevelt's body.

Then I make a decision. Aunt Jane is the first person I tell when she calls this morning before school. "Eleanor Roosevelt is going to be my Great Face."

"Wonderful!" Aunt Jane says. Then she's off to teach a class, and I catch the bus.

Later, in history, Marty leans across the aisle and points to a German soldier in my history book. "My family is from Germany. During World War Two the Germans wanted my grandpa to come back and fight for them, but he said, 'Hell, no.' I want to visit someday. Have you ever been there?"

"No," I say. Marty frowns, as if he's disappointed, and turns away.

"My ancestors are from Australia. Our family raised kangaroos in the outback, but we also used to be fishermen off the Great Barrier Reef. Giant swordfish and barracudas. My great-grandfather once killed a huge shark that was terrorizing the coast. He was a big hero. They even have a day named after him."

Marty leans across his desk, eyes wide. "Really? When's the day?"

I blurt out, "The third Wednesday in June."

"That's so cool," he says, nodding. He really means it.

I think about this later when Grace asks me after lunch, "How's Abby?"

Why is she asking about Abby? What have I said about her? I worry that Mrs. Hollis told her about the ulcer attacks. Did Marty tell her what I said about our family? Then I remember what I told her about the stomach flu. "Getting better."

"Is she okay?"

"We took her to the hospital." Why do I say this? A hundred nerves sting my face.

"She must have been so scared. Poor thing." I nod and lick my lips. Grace drops her eyes. "Why didn't you tell me? Aren't we friends?"

"Well, of course we're friends!"

It's all I worry about for the rest of the day. I don't want to talk about my family, but I don't want to tell Grace any more tall tales, either. One day she's going to find out who I really am, and then she's not going to want to be friends with me.

I'm the first one home today. I sit in front of our

Christmas tree. I reach for the plastic Santa on the coffee table and turn the crank. Santa sways on the table as he sings, "Here comes Santa Claus, here comes Santa Claus." I crank him up, and he does it again.

I wish our tree had big colored bulbs instead of little flashing ones. I wish our kitchen smelled like cinnamon, that we had hand-stitched stockings and an evergreen wreath on the front door and Christmas cards sent to us from friends all over the country.

"I'm off to the store," Mom said the other night. We were cleaning the kitchen. Dad was watching TV. She glanced at him. "Everything's okay here, don't you think?"

I stood in the doorway and watched her hurry down the driveway. The flashing red lights on our Christmas tree gave her a reddish tint as they shone through the window and lit up her back. She turned and looked back at me.

"Can you think of anything else we need?"

"How about some of those little chocolate milk boxes?" Sometimes Grace and I have two or three when we're in her room.

"Sure, and while I'm at it I'll get some lobster and caviar."

When I turned back, Teddy was watching me. "That's what you have at Grace's?"

I shrugged.

Now I crank up the Santa again. I'll have to be careful what I say about Grace in front of Teddy.

Chapter 28

Emily hasn't shown up at the rendezvous spot. Samantha is worried.

This isn't like her. Samantha sits on the steps and thinks. What could have happened to Emily? Then a strange feeling overtakes her, and Emily's face pops into her mind. Samantha feels a great pain through her head, as if she's being electrocuted.

Something is wrong. She sees darkness and feels a chill tingle up her back. What does this mean? She stands up. Emily is in trouble. Samantha is going to have to find her.

Chapter 29

There are many rules to learn in this school.

For example, girls who play sports always sit together on the far side of the cafeteria. School clubs, such as the newspaper and choir, are considered geeky, but band is not. And Roxanne and Ariel don't talk to Jennifer Conway and her friends, and vice versa.

Roxanne tells me these things one day during lunch.

"Why don't you and Jennifer talk?" I ask Roxanne.

She glances at Ariel and then turns to me, smirking. "Let's just say that there was a certain boy last year . . ."

"Joey Paxon," Ariel whispers.

". . . who liked me a little more than someone else we know." Roxanne and Ariel start giggling together.

"Who is Joey Paxon?"

"Old news, old news." Roxanne waves her hand at me as she and Ariel keep laughing.

Are all middle schools like this, or just ours?

Jennifer Conway talks to me all the time now, since the day the interview came out. "Great job on the article," she whispered to me in the lunch line.

Lately Jennifer hasn't said anything about the interview, but she still says hi. In history. In the hallway. I say hi back and in my head beg her not to bring up the interview. What would everyone say if they knew I'd made it up?

One night on the phone I ask Grace about Roxanne's rules.

"I guess there are cliques," she says. "But I try to be nice to everyone."

The other day she spent the lunch hour talking to George Martins, the guy with the clubfoot. "You're friends with everyone. Even George."

"I feel sorry for him because he's got this muscle disease that his dad and his dad's dad have. And I feel sorry for people like Hannah because she's never had anything bad happen to her, so she doesn't get what people have to go through sometimes."

"Yeah, but what if someone is mean?" I ask.

"I can't get mad at them."

But I didn't say anything about getting mad at anyone. "I don't think you have to be mad at that person. Maybe you just don't like them anymore."

Grace is quiet for a moment. "I want to look at people's good sides. That way I won't get angry. I don't know why, but I just don't ever, ever want to be mad at anyone."

I remember how snotty Jennifer was at the newspaper meeting. And even though she says hi to me now, she does it because of what I wrote. I don't really like her, but I'm not angry at her. I'm not sure why Grace doesn't like to be mad at people, but it's no wonder everyone likes her. It's no wonder she has so many friends.

Christmas is in one week and that means Uncle Terry and Aunt Jane will be here soon. After school let out yesterday I checked out a couple of books about Eleanor Roosevelt so I'll be ready to talk to Aunt Jane about her.

Eleanor was the first first lady to have a job, write for a newspaper, and talk on the radio. She also tried to get equal rights for black people and better conditions for the women working in factories.

Tonight I sit at the table with my books and my sketchbook while Dad does the crossword puzzle. It's something to watch him; it takes him only a few minutes. Except on Sundays, when he says they're harder. Then it takes him fifteen minutes.

"The Roosevelts call their house Hyde Park." I look up. "Where's that?"

"On the Hudson River, north of New York City. Actually, the house is on an estate called Springwood that's in the town of Hyde Park."

"Who lives there now?"

"No one, I believe. It's a landmark. You know, open to the public."

"Did you ever go there with your family?" I glance at him but he doesn't answer. "How do you know about this?"

He looks at me over the top of his glasses. Then he grins this sneaky grin, as if he's going to let me in on a secret. I lean back. He points to his head. "You know what it is. You've got it, too. This ability to remember things. You're just like me."

I frown. Dad acts as if we're part of a club that no one else is allowed to join.

Chapter 30

Dr. Bennett offers jobs to Grace and me. Once a week we're going to clean his waiting room and receptionist's area at his dentist's office, and he'll pay us ten dollars each. Mom says it's ironic that I found a job before her. Teddy says he wants a job, too. Abby says, "Now there'll be *another* day after school when you're not home."

On Tuesday afternoons Dr. Bennett always closes at three, and today Grace lets us in the office with her key. We find the cleaning supplies in the closet, and we start in the waiting room. After a few minutes Grace stops dusting and tells me a story.

"My grandparents had this big white sheepdog named Peek-a-Boo. He was wild and slept in a pen behind the swimming pool. But Grandpa loved him. Once winter came, they argued about where he'd sleep. Finally Grandma gave in and let Peek-a-Boo sleep in their bedroom if Grandpa promised to take him out at night.

"Well, the first night everything went okay and Grandpa let Peek-a-Boo out only once. The next two nights Grandpa didn't need to let him out at all.

"On the fourth night Peek-a-Boo woke up whimpering. Grandma nudged Grandpa until he got up. He said to Peek-a-Boo, 'Just a minute while I take care of my business.' Then he went into the bathroom and shut the door. Peek-a-Boo couldn't wait. He jumped onto the bed on Grandpa's side, peed, jumped down, and curled up in the corner.

"When Grandpa saw that Peek-a-Boo was asleep, he decided the whimpering was a false alarm. Grandma had to put the pillow over her head to hide her laughing. When he climbed into bed and realized what had happened, he shot up, screaming."

By the time she finishes this story, I've dusted the entire room by myself. But I don't care. I'm laughing so hard the time just flies by.

Tonight I dig through the boxes in the basement, looking for my snow pants. Dad is at his workbench, happy. So I ask him questions—Why does this screw go here? What is that orange thingy on the engine? Then, "Do you have any stories about your dad?"

"Nah."

"Didn't anyone tell you any stories about him?"

Poppy died in a car accident when Dad was fourteen. He owned a hardware business. I learned these things from Mom because Dad won't talk about him.

Dad sets an engine carefully on the bench and reaches for a different one. It takes so long for him to answer that I think he's forgotten the question.

"Nah. Regular guy. Did regular things."

It's as if Dad never even had a life before us.

Chapter 31

Snow falls today. Big fluffy wet flakes that stick to everything—the street, the trees, the cars, our coats, our hair. Grace loves snow, and on the way to her house she makes me stop in *every* yard on her street to make snow angels. We "grace" ten front yards before we get to this grouchy old lady's house. She's shoveling.

We have to grace Mrs. Halligan's yard. We ask, and she waves her shovel at us and tells us to go away. Grace grabs me and we run up the woman's driveway and into her yard and make angels. The woman yells and starts after us, and we laugh hysterically as we run away.

When we get to Grace's, Carollyn is in the kitchen. We make popcorn and mugs of hot chocolate and sit at the counter. Grace tells her about the snow angels and how Mrs. Halligan yelled at us. Carollyn says it's too bad people are so set in their ways that they can't accept a gift when they're handed one. I hadn't thought of it like that.

Then Carollyn brings out a tin of cookies she's made, and I take two and set them in front of me. Grace doesn't want any. I'm admiring the different colors of frosting on the cookies and listening to Carollyn talk about how this recipe has been passed down from her relatives in Germany, when Grace leaves.

I don't know where she's gone, but as I start eating my snowman I think about what Grace's mom's lemon cookies must have tasted like. Carollyn's cookies are great. But maybe it's hard for Grace to eat these when she's thinking about her mom.

Grace is in her room, drawing snowflakes and angels in her sketchbook. I sit next to her. I lick the frosting off my lips, and suddenly I feel guilty about eating Carollyn's cookies. Is Grace mad at me for this? But maybe she's just sad.

Should I go home? "Are you okay?"

"Yeah."

I wipe my hand across my face, making sure the frosting is gone. I reach for a pen and draw a stick figure of a woman carrying a shovel. Then Grace colors the woman's hair gray, like Mrs. Halligan, and pretty soon we're laughing.

Later, as I get ready to leave, Grace walks me to the door. I stand in the doorway and look back at her in the house. It's so cold that I see my breath under the porch light.

"You're so lucky to have such a great family," I say.

She gets this look on her face, like she smells something burning in the kitchen. "But I don't have my mom. Carollyn isn't my mom."

How could I have said such a dumb thing?

When I get home, Abby is at the door. "I've been waiting for you for hours."

She shows me a page from a magazine. *Girl rescues cat*, reads the caption underneath a picture of a girl standing in front of a giant beech tree, hugging a cat. "Aunt Jane sent this to me."

But it's not until I pull out the Popsicle sticks and start to make a castle that she finally smiles. Mom sits across from us, watching.

I wouldn't know what to do if something happened to her.

Chapter 32

Ariel and Roxanne are arguing. They stop when I sit. But Ariel's cheeks are still puffy and red, and her hands are on her hips. Roxanne keeps batting her black eyelashes.

"It's *so* annoying when you do that with your eyes," Ariel says. Then she storms off to the bathroom.

Roxanne pushes away from the table. "She's so moody. Don't you think she's, like, the moodiest person? You can't even talk to her."

She's right. Sometimes when I pass Ariel in the hall, she won't look at me. Then the next day she's nice to me, as if nothing had happened.

I look for Grace, but she's still talking to Mr. Parker, the lunchroom monitor. What can they possibly be talking about for fifteen minutes?

I turn back around. "Why were you arguing with Ariel?"

Roxanne stabs a toothpick into her sandwich. "Now I can't even remember!"

After Ariel returns, the three of us eat. When Roxanne sighs and walks off, Ariel leans across her tray to me. "What did she say about me?"

If she and Roxanne can talk using brain waves, doesn't she already know? I keep chewing.

Ariel huffs and crosses her arms. "Don't believe her. She's evil. I honestly, truly believe that she's evil. And I can say this because I've known her my whole entire life."

If I had a cousin who was also my best friend, I'd never want to argue with her like this.

"She's miserable, too," Ariel says. "Can't you tell? She desperately wants to be friends with Jennifer's group. It's disgusting. Why would you want to be friends with that brainless crowd? And what would they want with *her*?"

I don't answer because Roxanne comes back. They both stare at me but no way will I say anything. Besides, Roxanne doesn't seem miserable or desperate about anything except maybe Ariel.

Later I'm surprised to see them laughing together in the hall. Do they argue and make up like this all the time? It must be pretty nice to know that even if you fight, your best friend is still going to be there.

Chapter 33

On Christmas morning Dad sits cross-legged on the floor, passing out presents. He wears gym shorts, a Detroit Tigers T-shirt, and a red Santa hat.

"This gift is designated for Abigail Summers," Dad says in an English accent.

Abby skips toward him. He pulls her legs and she collapses, laughing, on his lap. Then he gives her a noogie as she tears into her present. It's a two-hundred-piece My Faire Princess Magic Bus. Abby squeals. "Just what I wanted!"

When it's my turn, I take my present from Dad without being caught.

When Dad calls Mom's name, she falls into his lap before he even reaches for her. They laugh and roll on the floor, ripped Christmas paper clinging to their pajamas. Abby and I look at each other. When I smile, Abby smiles back. Teddy sits on the couch, listening to music through his headphones and staring out the window.

Later I find Mom circling ads in the paper. In the past three months she's applied for a few positions, but no one has called. Too many people are out of work, she says.

"I like working," Mom says now. "I miss it."

I like it when Mom works, too. We had fun when she took us to Take Our Daughters and Sons to Work Day two years ago. Teddy, Abby, and I sat at an empty desk next to her, playing with bandages and cotton balls while she answered phones. Everyone called her Mrs. Summers, which sounded important and official.

"What's been your favorite job?" I know she worked in a plant and in a printing shop. Two years ago she got fired from that job at the doctor's office because she missed so many days staying home with us when Dad was drinking.

"Oh, the plant." She smiles and takes a sip of eggnog.

"Because you met Dad?"

"Lots of reasons. Mostly because it was my first real job. I was seventeen when my dad died, and then I did odd jobs for two years, living with my mom, saving money. One day I packed up, got on a bus, and went to Detroit. With no job and not knowing a soul and only four hundred dollars in my pocket. Talk about taking a chance! I hardly believe I did it." She shudders but smiles and goes back to the newspaper.

"I bet your mom missed you." I'm not sure this is true. She rarely talks about her.

"I don't know. We didn't get along so good. Her ulcers made her such a grouch. She'd say to me, you'll never leave. We'd argue, and I'd threaten to leave the next day. But it was scary, the thought of leaving home. Then one day I just did it."

Up in Teddy's room hundreds of pieces of Abby's bus are on his floor, and he's trying to put it together. When he got his pirate ship for Christmas years ago, he worked on it for days. But I think he'll have this bus done in no time.

I'm sure Mom's bus was nothing like this, with pink curtains, a wading pool on the roof, and a side that folds out into a tent. But when you do something as brave as she did, I guess what the bus looks like doesn't really matter.

Chapter 34

The next morning the doorbell rings while we're still in our pajamas. Dad has gone to work. Teddy is asleep. Abby and I follow Mom to the door. She holds her robe together at her throat and opens the door just a crack.

A woman and a young girl stand on our stoop. The girl thrusts a box of candy canes toward Mom. The woman wears a red parka with fur around the hood. She has a round face and a huge mouth with a gazillion teeth. She's so big and tall that she seems to take up the entire stoop.

"Thought we'd introduce ourselves," the woman says in a deep, booming voice. "I'm Shawna. This is Natalie. The two of us are renting the house across the street."

Mom thanks her and then introduces us. Abby wiggles her way past me so she's up front. The two girls are the same size. They stare at each other. I glance at their house. It seems just like ours, only the brick is lighter and the garage is on the other side.

"Off to work," Shawna says. "Can't dillydally. Just wanted to be neighborly."

We watch from the window as they hurry down the

sidewalk and climb into their car. Shawna speeds off down the street.

"I haven't heard anyone say 'dillydally' in years." Mom chuckles. "Funny. She didn't say anything about a husband. Maybe it's just the two of them."

She stares at Shawna's house.

In the afternoon Abby and Natalie build a snowman in Natalie's front yard. Only it looks like the snowman has a tail and is lying down.

"It's not a snowman, it's a snow bunny!" Abby says later, her cheeks red and raw from the cold. Mom and I laugh.

Now Abby has a friend, too.

Chapter 35

Aunt Jane is tall with shiny, curly blond hair that falls in bunches down her back. Her shoulders fill her sweaters until there doesn't seem to be one millimeter of space left. They're the first thing you notice about her.

Her shoulders are so big because she swam the butterfly stroke in college. In the butterfly, swimmers reach out above their heads, pull the water, flick their feet and bring their arms up over their heads again. You have to be superstrong to do this.

Aunt Jane has a way of talking to people, like Carollyn does, that makes you feel as if you're the most important person in the world. From the moment she arrives, I follow her around and tell her almost everything.

"Are you and Grace going to make your book into a series?"

She says "Grace" casually, as if she knows her, as if Grace has always been a part of our lives. I feel a tingle up my back. I watch Aunt Jane place her sweaters on my desk. She puts her running shoes and a pair of boots under my bed.

"We're thinking five more books, maybe ten," I say, holding my sleeping bag. Even though I haven't thought much beyond this book, a series sounds pretty great. Aunt Jane smiles and nods. Maybe I could write twenty books.

I follow her into the kitchen, and Mom asks her to peel potatoes. I shift my feet and watch. I want her to keep asking me questions.

Outside Dad, Abby, and Uncle Terry play football. Uncle Terry is taller and thinner than Dad, but the hair on his head, his arms, and the backs of his hands is as black as Dad's. He even stands like Dad, hands on his hips and feet apart. I watch Uncle Terry throw Dad to the ground, then raise his arms. They're laughing.

Teddy should be out there but he's in his room. I run up and knock on his door. When he doesn't answer I push it open. He's on his bed, staring at the ceiling, listening to loud, screaming music.

"Is dinner ready?" He turns down the music.

I shake my head and sit next to him. When we were little, people used to think we were twins. But now his face is longer and his hair is darker and wilder.

"Uncle Terry and Dad are outside playing football with Abby," I say.

Teddy shrugs and looks away. I've told him a hundred times that it could have been me or Abby who slipped up with Uncle Terry. We were playing kickball with the neighbors. Uncle Terry was passing through on his way to Chicago for business. We thought it was so funny that he wanted to play in his suit and tie. When it was his turn, Uncle Terry raced up to the ball, kicked, and completely missed it.

"Try again." Teddy threw the ball back to the pitcher. "You can do it. At least you're not drunk."

Uncle Terry laughed, but his eyes flickered, and Teddy and I both saw it. Later, when he and Dad went into the basement, we knew what they were talking about.

I look around at Teddy's empty walls, and then I watch him pull on the hairs on his chin. "You can't stay up here forever."

"I want to listen to this." He turns up the volume.

At dinner Uncle Terry taps his fork against his water glass and stands.

"Merry Christmas." He raises his water glass. "Congratulations to my big brother on his new job. He may be the smartest, but I'm the best-looking in the family."

Everyone laughs. Dad grabs Uncle Terry's arm and punches it. But he's smiling. There's a look in Dad's eyes—like the times he apologizes.

I eat until I'm stuffed, and I laugh as Dad and Uncle Terry tease each other. I talk about my Great Faces project. I ask Uncle Terry about his job. Abby sings a song she learned. This is what a family is like, sitting around, telling stories.

I know Dad won't drink or lose his temper with them here, so I say, "What were Christmases like when you were kids?"

"I guess like this." Uncle Terry hesitates. "With a tree and presents."

He looks at Dad, who fiddles with the saltshaker. Dad glances at him, his lips pinched together. Maybe Dad hated his life growing up. But he doesn't hate Uncle

Terry. Uncle Terry could be the only person he really likes.

"When can we open the presents you brought?" Abby asks.

"Abby," Mom says. "After dinner."

Uncle Terry glances at Teddy, and Teddy kind of smiles back. I don't think Uncle Terry knew then, or even knows now, how mad Dad was at Teddy after Uncle Terry had that talk with Dad in the basement.

"Why did Uncle Terry say I told him?" Teddy cried to me that day, tears streaming down his cheeks, when he finally came upstairs. *"Why?"*

It was at least four months until Dad finally talked to Teddy. All that time Teddy sat on the basement stairs and watched Dad build his planes. And sat on the stoop while Dad washed his truck. And sat in the yard while Dad grilled. Finally Teddy gave up.

"Let's open presents now." Dad stands and begins stacking dinner plates. Uncle Terry's smile fades as he looks from me to Dad. Why can't we talk about anything?

We go to the living room and sit near the tree. I sit next to Aunt Jane.

"There's something we want to tell you," Uncle Terry says. "Jane has been offered a visiting professorship in Hong Kong. They've offered me a job teaching in the law school. It's unusual that we'd both get offers."

"You're moving to China?" Dad asks.

"Just for two, maybe three years," Aunt Jane says. "We leave in late summer." She puts her hand on my knee and holds it there.

Three years? My shoulders sink. Aunt Jane squeezes my knee.

"Congratulations," Dad says.

"Oh my, yes," Mom says. *"Hong Kong."*

Uncle Terry and Aunt Jane give me a book about the Roosevelts. I say thanks and flip through the pages. I should be happy for them. But I sneak away after we clean up and crawl under my bed. I stick my finger in a hole in the box spring and let it hang, half in, half out. I smell the leather from Aunt Jane's boots next to me.

At the airport last summer she said, "If your dad can't take care of you, you have to take care of yourself." Aunt Jane isn't going to be able to take care of me, either.

But I can take care of myself.

I pull my finger through the hole and take a bunch of fabric with me. The tear is sharp and loud but I like how clean and smooth it feels.

The next day Aunt Jane and I go for a walk. We stop in front of Grace's house. The white lights are on in the bushes, and there are newspapers stacked on the porch. Grace went to her grandmother's and won't be home until after New Year's.

"She has a gazillion relatives," I say. "And they get together for everything."

"Does that make you think of your family?" Aunt Jane wears a big brown coat and a white knit hat that stops just above her ears.

"Yeah, I guess."

Aunt Jane looks back at the house. "You know, Terry doesn't talk about it much, either. I think it's too painful."

"What do you mean?" I want her to keep talking.

"Poppy was difficult when they were growing up. After he died, their mom, Louise, was so . . . how should I say . . . demanding. Terry says your dad got the brunt of everything. I think Terry feels very indebted to him. Does your dad ever talk about this?"

"No." I can tell she knows more. "What else does he say?"

"You should ask your dad about this."

"He won't talk. I never even met Grandma Louise."

Aunt Jane pinches her lips together. "I have an old trunk of hers in our attic. Maybe there are some pictures in it I could send you."

I nod.

"You should ask him. See if he'll talk about this. It would be good for him." She pauses and lowers her voice. "Is he drinking?"

She tilts her head and looks at me. I curl my hands into fists and turn to Grace's house. A lamp is on in the living room next to the bookshelf. I know that lamp. It's small with yellow flowers on the shade. Grace's grandmother gave it to them.

"No." I know she's waiting for me to talk more about this, so I say the first thing that comes to my mind. "Hong Kong is so far away."

Aunt Jane nudges her shoulder into mine. "It is. But we'll be back to visit. And we'll write to each other. Are you worried about that?"

"No!" I laugh as if to say, *What? Me?* It's easy not to tell the truth, because if you think about it, how will she know? She's not around enough to see the stuff Dad does. And now she's going to be even farther away.

"Maybe we'll get back for Christmas next year," she says. "And we'll try to see you in the spring. I'm speaking at a conference in Ann Arbor. Maybe we could stop by when it's over."

I turn back to Grace's house. I think about Brianna and Mary Rose and the other people I knew in the towns where we've lived. Right after you move, you think about them a lot. But as the months go by, you pretty much forget them. And they forget you.

"I'm worried about going away, too, Meg. We'll both have to work extra hard at staying in touch. Okay?"

I smile a little and nod.

I'll be okay, I tell myself. But I know how busy Aunt Jane is. And Hong Kong is halfway around the world.

I pull back my shoulders, and we start for home.

Chapter 36

It's Middle School Night at the YMCA, and it's packed. Grace passes me the basketball, it hits my foot, and we trip over each other as we chase it. Then we're on the floor, laughing crazily, our legs tangled together.

"Get up," Marty yells, "or get out of the way if you're not going to play." We stay where we are. The boys play around us, and this is even funnier. We can't stop laughing.

Finally we get up and go into the racquetball court, where it's quiet. We hit the ball a few times, but pretty soon we lie in the middle of the floor and chew a pack of gum and talk about the newspaper, Christmas presents, and the ending of our book.

I could stay here all night. Then Grace asks, "What's Teddy doing tonight?"

Something flutters in my stomach. She turns to me, waiting. "How come you never talk about anybody in your family?"

"There's nothing to say. Regular people. They do regular things."

"You must think I'm such a blabbermouth." Her cheeks redden. "I'm always talking about everything all the time."

"No, I love talking to you. It's my favorite thing in the world."

"Really?"

"Yes, of course!"

"Good, me too." She sighs loudly.

Afterward Grace and I catch a ride with Jennifer's mom. Cars line both sides of Grace's street, and every light in her house is on. I stiffen. Grace said her dad and Carollyn were having a party, but I had no idea there would be so many people.

People are in the dining room, kitchen, living room, and pantry. A man plays the piano and a group stands behind him, singing. It's loud and warm. Someone laughs from the other room. How do they know so many people? I jam my hands in my pockets.

"Meggers!"

Dr. Bennett waves to me. He comes over and hugs Grace and then me. I take my hands out of my pockets and smile. He has nicknames for everyone. Grace is Scooter, Ricky is Ricky Ricardo, and now I have a nickname, too. *Meggers.*

"So, girls, what's happening in the newspaper world? Any scandals?"

Grace rolls her eyes.

"Someone broke into the principal's office and trashed it," I say.

101

His smile fades. "Really? What happened?"

"We don't know yet," I say. "This just happened the day before yesterday."

"How will you write about this?"

"What do you mean?"

"Will you investigate this on your own? Will you put this on the front page?"

Grace and I look at each other. Hardly anyone takes our newspaper seriously, and here he's telling us to be hotshot reporters.

"Melinda, wait." Dr. Bennett reaches for a woman and pulls her over to us. She's tall and thin and older than most people here. She kisses Grace on the cheek.

"This is Melinda, Grace's great-aunt," Dr. Bennett says to me. A man grabs his shoulder, and Dr. Bennett turns and laughs. Then the man hugs Grace, and she giggles.

"So nice to see Grace not so angry anymore," Melinda says to me. "I'm sorry, dear, I don't think I heard your name."

"Meg."

"Oh, you're the writer! I've heard so much about you. At Christmas Grace told me all about your book. I can't wait to read it."

I feel my back straightening, my shoulders rising. "Well, it's not done yet."

She winks at me. "Keep writing."

My feet aren't touching the ground. That's what it feels like as Grace and I make our way to the kitchen.

All around me people are laughing, smiling, talking. I want to meet them all. I want to listen to their stories and the questions they ask each other.

We fill our plates with crackers and cheese and little breaded things that Grace calls shrimp puffs. We walk halfway up the stairs and sit. From our perch above the party, we can see the living room, the entrance hall, and into the dining room.

"There are so many people here," I say. "And they're having so much fun."

Grace wrinkles up her forehead. "They're silly. When they get together they act so stupid. Aren't your parents and their friends like that?"

I eat a shrimp puff even though I don't like it much. I chew for a long time. "Yeah, I guess it's just different when it's not your parents."

Grace nods. We watch Carollyn cross the living room. She noses her way into groups, offering a dish of food, laughing. She's dressed in a long skirt and a turtleneck. Her hair is piled on top of her head, and wisps of it fall down the sides of her face. She and Aunt Jane are the coolest women I've ever met.

"At least Carollyn never lied to me," Grace says. "That's one good thing."

"Who lied to you?" I spit the words out. My cheeks burn.

"Everybody." Grace stares at Carollyn. "My mom didn't wear her hair like that."

"What did her hair look like?"

"It was blond. No, kind of brown. Brownish blond."

"You must really miss her."

"People don't ask me about her anymore. It's not like I want to talk to everyone. But you're the only one who ever asks me questions about her. It's like everyone is afraid to talk to me. It's like she didn't even exist. Does this make sense?"

I nod, and she looks so relieved that I keep nodding.

Chapter 37

"You'll never get away with this," Samantha tells the robber.

"What are you going to do about it?" He laughs an evil laugh. Samantha's arms and legs are tied with rope. She tries to wiggle free but she can't. The robber finishes digging. He drops the bag of jewels into the hole and then covers it up.

"I'll be back to get this when the coast is clear," he says. "Then I'll figure out what to do with you."

When he's gone, Samantha closes her eyes and concentrates. "Emily, Emily, Emily. Hear me. Come and save me."

Chapter 38

Today Mr. Holcomb tells us that for our Great Faces project we have to write a four-page report and read it out loud. Over the years students have been creative in their presentations. Some have written poems. Others have dressed up like their subjects.

When Mr. Holcomb turns to the blackboard, Marty leans over and says, "Your great-grandfather should be your Great Face. Wouldn't that be so cool?"

At first I don't know what he's talking about. Then I remember. "I can't do that."

"Why not? He's famous enough. There's a day named after him. Right?"

"But he was really . . . private and secretive. We don't know much about him."

Marty shakes his head. "Go on the Internet. I bet there's lots of stuff. Or tell Mr. Holcomb. He'll help you."

I grip the bottom of my chair so hard that I can't feel my fingers. I look up, and Mr. Holcomb is in front of us. "Is there something you two would like to share with us?"

Marty looks as if he's about to say something, so I cut in. "No. Nothing."

Only when Mr. Holcomb starts talking to the class do I take my hands off my chair. It's easy making these things up, too easy. Then I'm stuck with them.

Chapter 39

After school Grace and I clean Dr. Bennett's office. I start by dusting the receptionist's area, and Grace decides to take the waiting room. After ten minutes I peek through the door. Grace is on her knees, drawing at the kids' table.

I frown because this has been happening a lot. I seem to do most of the cleaning. Last week I cleaned the bathroom all by myself, including the toilet.

Grace sees me and giggles. "Let's put this on his desk!" She holds up a piece of paper. She has cut Dr. Bennett's head off one of his brochures and taped it to the paper. Under the head she drew a huge body with an arm holding a pair of pliers.

It's really good, and I can't help laughing. We charge down the hall. Dr. Bennett is very neat and doesn't want us to clean his office, so we hardly come in here. Grace lays the drawing on his desk. My eyes stop on the framed photos by the window. Carollyn. Grace and Ricky. A woman with blond hair and blue eyes: Grace's mom.

Then I see a photo of Grace and me, taken at one of our sleepovers. I'm looking to the side. But Grace smiles at the camera with her beautiful white teeth. "Look at this!"

Grace glances at it. "Oh, I know. My dad loves this picture."

I take a deep breath and look at it some more. How cool is it that I have a place on his shelf, next to Grace?

Chapter 40

Two nights later everything happens fast.

"You say that again!" Dad reaches for Teddy and grabs the front of his shirt. Up go Teddy's fists, sometimes connecting with Dad's head but mostly blocked by Dad's arms. Dad pushes him against the wall. They're yelling and swearing.

"Stop this!" Mom is between them, pushing Teddy away with her hip, pulling at Dad's arms. Abby stands on a chair and screams. I barely know what I'm doing— pulling at my hair, mumbling, trying to get my feet to move. Do something! But I'm paralyzed.

Then there's a crack, and Mom staggers and falls against the refrigerator. Dad lets go of Teddy. Mom grabs her nose, and blood streams onto her hands. My body goes numb. I can't believe how much blood there is, how red it looks.

But something about the blood wakes me. "See what you've done!"

My voice comes from some other place inside me. The room darkens. My body shakes. *I'm going to throw up*. Teddy pulls me into the living room. I take a deep breath.

"I didn't do it," Dad calls from the kitchen. "It isn't my fault. Don't blame me."

He hides in the kitchen. Coward.

Mom lies on the couch. Abby kneels next to her and holds Mom's hand. With the end of my shirt I dab at the blood and tears. Teddy goes to the kitchen for an ice pack and comes back biting his lip, squeezing his cheeks, trying not to cry. This scares me more than Mom's nose.

"It's okay, Teddy, it's okay, it was an accident," Mom says.

"But it was my elbow." Teddy pulls the back of his hand across his eyes.

"I know, but it was an accident. It doesn't hurt. Really, it doesn't."

But later I hear her still crying in her bedroom. She stares at herself in the mirror—first from one side, then from the other, then straight on. She pushes her nose, trying to make it straight again.

"Do you want more ice?" I try to make my voice steady. Ice, aspirin, Pepsi—anything! Just be happy. Don't cry. *Please!* "Should we go to the hospital?"

"No, I'll be okay. It doesn't hurt." She cries and pushes her nose around.

I slide down the wall and sit on the floor. With my fingers I try to hold on to the carpet. But the shag is too short and I can't get a good grip. If I could, I'd rip these threads right out of the carpet.

An hour later Dad skulks around the corner. I try to grab the carpet.

"She's all right?" He's drinking coffee, sobering up.

111

"No, she's got a broken nose!" My face burns as I stare at the wall.

"But she'll be okay?" When I don't answer, he turns back to the living room.

Dr. Bennett wouldn't be drunk or slap Grace or call Carollyn an idiot or call Ricky a runt. Dr. Bennett is amazing. And so is Carollyn.

When I'm at the Bennetts' I feel as if I could be an amazing person, too. There's something about the house—the winding staircase, the kitchen that always smells as if something yummy is cooking—that makes my heart race. Or maybe it's not the house. Maybe it's Carollyn and Dr. Bennett, who talk to me all the time. Or Grace. I don't know. I feel so ready to *be anything*.

Over there I'm not paralyzed.

When Mom finally comes out of the bedroom, her eyes and nose are puffy, but she's no longer crying. And she's put on some red lipstick. "I think it's not so crooked. Look, do you think it's crooked? Does it look bad? Tell me."

"It looks fine. You can't even tell."

She nods. That was one lie worth telling. But then something tightens across my chest. What if Grace finds out about all the other lies I've told this year?

Chapter 41

Aunt Jane has sent a box of pictures from Grandma Louise's cedar chest. There are a dozen pictures, and as I lift them out of the box I spread them on my floor.

In Grandma Louise's engagement picture, she wears pearls and the neck of her dress is cut in a sharp triangle. There are baby pictures of Dad and Uncle Terry. I stare at a picture of Dad. He's dressed in shorts and a shirt and tie, and his hair is plastered to his head. His knees have scabs. And he's scowling over his glasses at the camera.

I open a folded yellow newspaper. Poppy's picture is on the front page with a headline that reads LOCAL BUSINESSMAN DIES IN CAR CRASH. He had a heart attack while driving and was killed when his car hit a tree. The article lists all that Poppy did: Sigma Chi at University of Michigan, Outstanding Business Leader of the Year, hospital board member. *He leaves a wife, Louise Summers, and two children, Robert, 14, and Terence, 10.*

No wonder Dad looks so miserable. It must have been terrible for him when Poppy died. Like Grace. I look at the picture of Dad in his short pants. He was probably Abby's age. His dad hadn't died yet. So why was he so unhappy?

I pick up Grandma Louise's picture. Her hair is brown and wavy, like mine, and it flips over her ear just like mine. I face the mirror, holding the picture next to my cheek.

She's not looking straight at the camera, but off to the left. I look to the side like she does, but then I can't see the mirror. So I stand there for a while staring at us in the mirror while Grandma Louise stares out my bedroom window.

Chapter 42

Today in the library I put my head down, and the next thing I know the librarian shakes me. Where am I? The side of my mouth is wet. When I look down I see a drool spot in the middle of Eleanor Roosevelt's chest. I know Mrs. Petrila sees it too, because she gives me one of these snotty *you don't take care of your things, do you?* looks.

"I haven't been sleeping," I say. "I think I've got some kind of not-sleeping disease."

"Oh?" Her eyebrows arch.

"The doctors can't figure it out. Sometimes I don't sleep all night."

Her eyebrows fall and she clears her throat. I have to go for it now.

"Next summer I'm going to Cambridge to be part of this research group at Harvard that studies sleep patterns. I'm going to stay with my aunt and uncle in Boston."

Her eyebrows rise again. She squeezes my shoulder.

When she walks away I put my head down and try to make my body limp. But my chest is so tight I can barely breathe. I want to cry but I don't know why.

Chapter 43

We know by the way he comes in the door. How he thrusts his coat on the rack, as if daring it to fall off. Then without so much as a glance at us, he goes to the basement.

We get into our car at the same time Shawna and Natalie get out of theirs. Shawna waves and hesitates, as if she wants to come over. She and Mom have been talking a lot lately. But Mom drives away. And I think, Will Dad be angry that we've gone? Will he and Teddy fight when we get home? How will I finish my math homework at the mall?

We order French fries and Pepsis at the restaurant in Kmart. I'm amazed when the waitress gets our order right and sets the food in front of us. But none of us feel like eating. I pull out my sketchbook but I don't know what to write.

Mom wipes away tears with a tissue. Brown smudge marks come away. Today Mom covered her bruise with makeup before she went for a job interview. Before dinner she got a call saying that the job went to someone else.

"It's just as well," she said. "Seeing that your father is drinking again."

Now I watch her and say, "I wish we'd gone bowling."

I like how Mom says "Tough beans" when we throw gutter balls. But mostly I like how she floats down the lane, like a swan on water, and how when she lets go, the ball explodes and barrels into the pins.

"Meg!" Carollyn and Ricky wave from the entrance of the restaurant. My heart begins to pound as I look around. Too late to hide.

"This is a nice surprise!" Carollyn stands in front of us. She holds out her hand to Mom. "I'm Carollyn. This is Ricky."

"This is Grace's stepmom," I say. "And her brother."

"Oh." Mom shakes Carollyn's hand. She brings her other hand up to her face and shields her nose. "It's very nice to meet you. We hear so much about all of you."

"It's nice to meet you, too. I'm sorry we haven't met before this. But my, what a time you've had over the fall! The stomach flu is such an awful thing to have."

I jump in. "This is Teddy and Abby."

"Hi," Abby says. Teddy jams his hands in his pockets.

"So, what are you doing here?" I try to make my voice sound calm. What if Ricky mentions the things I told him about our Christmases?

"Ricky needs new shoes." Carollyn glances at my sketchbook and then my face. She looks extra long at Mom. Does she see the bruise?

I want Carollyn to go. I don't want her to ask where Dad is. I can't look at her. My throat throbs as she stands there.

"I guess we'll be off," Carollyn says finally. "It was nice to meet you."

"You, too." Mom smiles through her hand. They walk toward the entrance. Carollyn opens the door for Ricky and waves before disappearing. Something rips through my heart. I want to go with them.

And what will she tell Grace?

Teddy frowns at me. "What was she talking about? What stomach flu?"

I lick my lips. "Grace keeps wanting to come over."

They look at me.

"And you didn't want her to meet Dad?" Mom asks. When I nod, she bursts into tears. Abby stops playing with the ketchup she poured on her plate. Teddy looks from me to Mom. I sink into my chair.

"Don't be mad. I know I shouldn't have lied. I'm sorry."

Mom shakes her head. "I'm not mad. You shouldn't have to feel ashamed. You shouldn't have to be so afraid."

I sit up. What would it feel like not to be so afraid?

The next day I wait for Grace to say something. Did Carollyn notice Mom's nose?

"Carollyn said she saw you last night," Grace says finally in the lunch line.

"We were shopping."

Grace looks at me.

"Mom tripped and hurt herself last week. We think she broke her nose."

"Is she okay?"

I nod. Grace sighs as we walk. I stare at my tray.

"I've never even met Teddy. When can I come over to your house?"

"You wouldn't like it. There's nothing to do. It's boring."

I can tell she's disappointed. But I don't know what to do.

Chapter 44

We've just finished a newspaper meeting, and Ariel is at a computer, reading over my article on the night janitor. The janitor was pretty funny and I liked writing it.

Ariel looks up at me and Grace. "I think it's ready to send to the editor in chief," she says. I nod and she presses the Send button. "It's pretty good."

"Thanks." I don't know what mood she's in, but I smile.

"Oh." Ariel huffs as she glances at the door. "Look who just walked in."

Jennifer Conway stands at the door and frowns. She hurries toward Grace as people move out of her way.

"There you are." She doesn't glance at me or Ariel. "I've been looking all over for you. Are you coming to my party on Saturday night or what?"

"Yeah, I'm coming," Grace says.

"Don't forget your ice skates." She raises her eyebrows at me as if she's surprised to see me, even though I've been here the whole time. "Hey, you should come, too. Grace, don't you think Meg should come? My dad is going to build a bonfire. It'll be a blast."

Grace smiles at me. "Yes! You should come."

I don't have ice skates, but I nod. Then Jennifer leaves. When I turn back, Ariel is staring at me.

"You're going to go?" Ariel's mouth falls open. "To Jennifer Conway's *house*?"

I shove my hands in my pockets and shrug. What's wrong with Jennifer's house? Maybe it's a mansion so big that I'll get lost. Maybe everyone will know each other except me, and I won't know what to do. But Grace will be there.

"It'll be fun," Grace says.

Chapter 45

Rain falls all day Saturday. The snow turns gray and grainy, and puddles form on the ice. All afternoon I watch from my window. I don't know how Jennifer will have her party. But Grace calls to say that we'll go anyway. And she found a pair of skates for me.

Aunt Jane and Uncle Terry send us a postcard from the Caribbean, where they're on vacation. *Wish you were here,* they write. They must meet a lot of interesting people in all the places they travel.

Abby sits on my bed and draws. Her castle is gray and black. A huge purple dragon breathes fire on the front door. "It's metal," Abby says, "so the door can't burn. But the dragon doesn't know this because the princess is *so* sneaky."

I don't tell her that fire can burn metal if it's hot enough. "What about a unicorn?"

"Teddy says unicorns don't care about princesses, so they can't save them."

We hear footsteps on the stairs, and Teddy stands at our door, hair wet from the rain. He sees my bag. "Where are you going?"

"She's going to a party," Abby says. "And *then* she's sleeping at Grace's."

"Again?" Teddy shifts his feet.

The rain stops by the time Mom takes me to Grace's. Teddy slouches against the side door, and Abby sits in the back next to me. Dad is drunk at home. After they drop me off, they're going to the mall. Mom pulls up to Grace's.

"Have a nice time," Mom says, but I don't get out. I should go with them. I shouldn't leave them.

Then I look at Grace's house. Every light must be on, that's how bright the windows are. I know that Carollyn will be cooking dinner, Ricky will be playing with LEGOs, and Grace will be drawing.

I remember how Teddy ran out the door when Pete and Harris came down the hill on their bikes. Sometimes you could hear them laughing all the way up the street. He never hesitated about going. He never seemed worried about all of us.

"Bye." I open the door and run. I take the stairs two at a time, and after I ring the bell, I turn and wave. When Grace opens the door, I rush inside.

Jennifer lives in a small house on Clear Lake. It's nice, with a fireplace and all, but after what Ariel said I expected Jennifer to live in a big house like Grace's.

Grace and I throw down our coats and head to the basement. I recognize almost everyone. They sit around a table covered with bottles of pop and bowls of pretzels and popcorn. I sit next to Grace. Everyone smiles at me, but maybe they think I shouldn't be here.

Jennifer and her mom stand off to the side.

"It's too wet and the wood is soaked," Jennifer's mom says.

"You promised, and now everyone is so disappointed. And why does *she* have to be here?" She points to a young girl on the other side of the table. She has a long brown ponytail like Jennifer's and wears a pink sweater. She must be Jennifer's sister.

"She can stay for a while." Jennifer's mom turns to leave.

Jennifer goes to the table.

"Well . . . No skating. No bonfire. But we can *still* have fun." Her bright, golden eyes travel around the table. The others watch her, nodding. Something about the way she stands there with her hands on her hips, smiling, makes me feel as if I'll do anything she says.

But then she points to her sister. "And you, *you're* not allowed to say anything."

Her sister's face doesn't move a muscle. I hug my arms to my chest. I can't imagine ever speaking to Abby like this.

Jennifer turns on the CD player, and music thunders through the room. Girls follow Jennifer to the other side of the room. She tries to get them to dance, although mostly they just stand there watching her. She throws herself around, crashes into Hannah, and falls onto the couch, giggling.

I look at Grace. She and the others laugh at Jennifer. I laugh, too, because no one seems to mind that I'm here and because Jennifer *is* funny. She makes her body bend and twist. Then she jumps on the couch and dives into the pillows on the floor. She squirms around like a snake.

After a while we sit on the floor and eat. Everyone talks at once. About a seventh-grade boy they like, somebody's party last year, other things I don't know about. But this is nice. Are all their parties like this?

Then Jennifer leans toward Grace and whispers something in her ear. They both fall back on top of each other, giggling. The others glance at them but keep talking. Except Hannah, who sits on the other side of Jennifer. Her sweater is just like Jennifer's only a shade lighter. She tugs at it and frowns.

"What's so funny?" Hannah grabs Jennifer's arm. "Come on, tell me. Who are you talking about? What's so funny?"

Jennifer snaps her arm away as she and Grace sit up.

"God, leave me *alone!*" Jennifer says. "Stop bugging me all the time!"

Hannah's lower lip quivers. Everyone starts talking again. I suck in my breath.

Jennifer sighs loudly and whispers in Hannah's ear. Hannah giggles and nods and smiles, her braces sparkling under the lights. But then Jennifer rolls her eyes when Hannah isn't looking.

After a while I go upstairs to use the bathroom. In the kitchen Jennifer is opening a bottle of pop. She smiles. "Are you having fun? I want you to have fun."

"Yeah."

She glances at the stairs and then lowers her voice. "You've lived all these different places, and here we are in boring Lake Haven, Indiana."

"No, it's nice." I bolt for the stairs. What stories did she hear? I've told so many.

In the basement Lisa tells us there are twenty-three days left until she goes to Costa Rica to visit her uncle. I look for Grace, but she's not here. I must have missed her upstairs.

"I've never even been out of the country," someone says.

"And I have to get all these shots," Lisa says. "You know, for diseases and stuff."

"Meg had malaria!" Hannah screams.

Everyone goes quiet and turns to me. Sweat breaks out under my arms.

"So, what was it like?" Lisa asks. "Was it really gross? Like puking and stuff?"

"What is malaria again?" Hannah asks.

"God, where did you go to get that?" someone asks me.

"You can die from malaria, you know," Lisa says.

Everyone is quiet again. My hands shake, so I jam them in my pockets.

"I don't remember much." I glance at the stairs and lick my lips. "Coming back from Boston last summer, this guy had a heart attack on our plane."

This isn't entirely true, but I did take a plane from Boston last summer. A man did get sick, he just didn't have a heart attack. But then everyone starts talking about plane trips and people getting sick. Maybe I'm off the hook.

But still I'm shaking. I sit at the table by myself. I practically jump off my chair when Grace puts her hand on my back and says, "What are they talking about?"

"I don't know." Please, *please* don't anyone say anything else.

Grace puts a tray of chocolate chip cookies on the table, and everyone dives into them. Jennifer's little sister reaches for two cookies, then retreats to the couch, where she watches. If Abby were here, she'd do the same thing. I picture Teddy slumped against the car door and Mom's hands on the steering wheel. They're probably home by now.

"You little pig!" Jennifer yells at her sister. "Who said you could have so many cookies? What are you still doing down here? Mom! Get the little pig out of here! *Mom!*"

Her sister eats her cookie slowly. Almost everyone else starts talking again and ignores them. Except Grace and me. I feel my heartbeat quicken.

Jennifer pushes her sister's shoulder. "Get out of here. No one wants you here, Miss Piggy. Put a cookie back. Mom, get Miss Piggy out of here!"

Somebody laughs. Then the music is back on and some of the girls are up again. I stand and walk to the couch. "She can have my cookie. I don't want one."

"Whatever." Jennifer jumps into the group and sings. I sit on the couch next to her sister. When Dad yells at

Abby, she usually holds my hand or puts her head on my shoulder.

"I like Oreos better than chocolate chip cookies." I hand her my cookie. She glances at me and shrugs. I look back at the girls. Grace has joined them. She just barely moves her hips and arms. But she's smiling and laughing.

Later, when we're in sleeping bags on Grace's floor, I ask, "Did you hear the way Jennifer talked to her sister?"

"She always does that. I feel sorry for Chris. But I feel sorry for Jennifer, too."

I lean on my elbow. It's dark, but I see Grace's face in the moonlight shining through the window. She's staring at the wall. "Why?"

Grace doesn't answer.

"She's kind of mean. I don't get why people like her." I lie back down.

"It just doesn't do any good to be mad at people," Grace says finally.

"Why? If people do things that aren't nice, it's okay to be mad at them." When Dad drinks, I hate him. Isn't that okay?

Grace is quiet.

She never says anything bad about anyone, and I've just talked about Jennifer. After she invited me to her party. But I can't find anything wrong with saying that something isn't right about how Jennifer treats people. I roll over and try to go to sleep.

No one is home when Carollyn drops me off in the

morning. After a half hour Abby and Mom come in. Abby runs to me.

"Natalie has a bunny!" she screams. "Her name is Marshmallow. She's so soft and white and cuddly. She let me hold her."

"We had coffee while the girls played," Mom says. "Shawna is from Alpena, only ten miles from where I grew up. We went to the same beach, the same places. I probably saw her at the bowling alley. Probably walked right past her. I'll be. Such a small world."

"Where's Dad?" I ask.

Mom throws her hands in the air. "Oh, I don't know. Somewhere. Home Depot."

I can't remember the last time I saw Mom smile like this.

Chapter 46

Tonight after dinner Dad is in the kitchen, waving a knife around, pulling everything out of the refrigerator—mayonnaise, butter, jelly, bologna.

"Let *me* make you the sandwich," Mom says. "You're going to get hurt."

He whirls around and points the knife in the direction of the coat stand. "See those new boots? They only cost me thirty-nine-ninety-five. In Michigan they would've been fifty bucks."

They're the same kind he's been wearing ever since I can remember—yellow construction boots with laces up the front. They stand at attention next to the door, the canvas shiny and unspotted. I smell our brownies in the oven.

"Bob, give me the knife," Mom says.

He mumbles something, and when he lays it on the counter, Mom takes it. Then Dad knocks the milk to the floor. He slips in it, and as he goes down he grabs the ashtray off the counter and pulls a gazillion cigarette butts with him to the floor.

I stand in the doorway, ready to push him facedown in the mess. Taste it!

"This is disgusting!" I yell. Abby starts to cry.

Mom points to the living room, but I don't move. Neither does Abby, even though the stove buzzer is going off and we can smell the brownies beginning to burn.

"Up, Bob, up," Mom says. He mumbles. She gets him into the bedroom, and Abby and I clean up the floor.

"You should've let him sleep there," I say when Mom comes back. The brownies will be fine when we cut away the burned parts along the edges.

"I can't do that," she says.

Maybe if she had left him there, he would have learned a lesson. Why does she always have to take care of him?

Teddy walks in, a paper bag in his arms. "What's wrong?"

"What took you so long?" Mom asks.

Teddy shrugs and puts the milk in the refrigerator. "I ran into this guy I know from school who works at the gas station next to the convenience store."

Teddy smiles at Abby. "Here, choose." He holds both arms behind his back. Abby points to his left arm, and he brings it around and hands Abby a small bag of M&M's. In his other hand he holds two bags, one for me and one for Mom.

"Thank you, thank you, *thank you!*" Abby says.

"What stinks?" he asks.

"We made these brownies for Natalie and Shawna, but we burned them because of *Dad,*" Abby says. "He was *drunk.*"

Teddy throws himself into a chair. The snow in his

131

hair drips onto his shoulders. His cheeks are red from walking in the cold.

"He's never going to stop drinking," Teddy says. "We should leave him."

I sit up. We look at Mom.

"And where would we go?" she says. "And what would happen to him?"

"Who cares about him?" Teddy crosses his arms. Abby pours out her M&M's and separates them by color. Mom stares off into the living room. Is she thinking about the last time she left somewhere, with only four hundred dollars in her pocket?

We jump when the phone rings. Teddy picks it up, says "Yeah" a couple of times, and then says, "Do you want to talk to Meg?" He hands me the phone and mouths, *Aunt Jane.*

"I just called to say hi. How's everything? What are you doing tonight?"

"Oh, just regular stuff. Homework. Abby and I made brownies."

"Yum. I bet they're good."

"Yeah." My ear starts to sweat against the phone.

Teddy jiggles the brownie pan. He tries to pry off a piece.

I turn away and stare at the door. There's no way for Aunt Jane to know what's really going on. I get ready for her next question, to make sure she doesn't hear anything in my voice to give us away.

Chapter 47

"So, was the party great, or what?" Roxanne asks me at lunch on Monday.

The party. It seems like it was a long time ago.

"It was okay." I almost tell them about how mean Jennifer was, but I know they don't like her, and why make it worse? I look for Grace. When I turn back, Ariel is staring at me.

"What did you do?" Roxanne asks.

"Listened to music. Regular stuff."

"I guess you'll start hanging out with them now." Ariel flips her hair behind her. I wait for her to laugh, but she's serious.

"They don't want to hang out with me. They only talked to me once all night."

Ariel and Roxanne look at each other, relieved, it seems. Now they're happy that everyone ignored me? I'll never figure this out.

Chapter 48

Carollyn picks Grace and me up after a basketball game. As we round the corner to my street, we see my house lit up like a Christmas tree. Mom is helping Teddy out the door. Abby stands without a coat in the middle of the frozen yard.

Carollyn pulls into the driveway and throws open her door, and a wall of cold rushes at me. I feel pinned to the seat, Abby's piercing screams filling my head. My legs go numb. Then Carollyn guides Teddy and Mom into the back next to me. Grace pulls Abby into the front seat with her.

Dad is in his robe at the front door, drunk. "Come back here! He's not hurt. Come back! Where are you going?"

Carollyn spins out of the driveway. I take a deep breath and turn to look. Part of me is terrified that Dad is racing after us, just about to reach for the car door, about to pull me out. About to swallow me up. Even as I watch him get smaller, a dark speck against the lit-up house, I can't get rid of this feeling.

"My arm really hurts," Teddy says. But his voice is calm. He isn't crying.

"Just keep still," Carollyn says. "We'll be at the hospital soon."

"I fell down the stairs," he says. I sink lower into the seat. I know he didn't fall. I glance at Mom. She holds her left hand to her temple, her eyes squeezed shut.

"It might be a fracture," Carollyn says. At a stoplight she turns to him. The streetlight shines through the window, and I see that look of concern on her face that I've seen before. Thoughts fire through my head. What happened? Could I have stopped this?

A doctor sees Teddy immediately because Carollyn knows everyone. She charges down the hall, Teddy on one side, Mom on the other. Grace, Abby, and I follow.

Teddy's X-ray shows a broken arm. The doctor who examines him is a woman. She's young, with long, thin fingers. She gently turns his arm from one side to the other. "It's a clean break, just below the elbow. He's lucky this isn't on the growth plate. It should heal nicely. What happened?"

"I fell down the stairs," Teddy says.

She glances at him, then back at his arm. "See this?" We look at the place she points to, halfway between his elbow and his shoulder. I see tiny clumps of spidery red veins.

"These are broken blood vessels," she says. "This happens when someone grabs you very hard and squeezes. You don't get these from falling down the stairs."

Teddy and Mom look at each other. I drop my eyes. *What happens in our family stays in our family.*

135

"I kind of got in a fight at school," Teddy says finally. "This guy grabbed me."

"Today?" she asks.

"Yeah." Teddy sits up straighter.

The doctor looks at Teddy and then at Mom. "We need to set this arm."

I stand over the doctor as she wraps first gauze pads and then strips of wet plaster over Teddy's arm. It takes only a few minutes. As we wait for it to dry, the doctor and Carollyn leave.

Out of the corner of my eye I see how Grace watches me. I don't look at her, because my face will give me away. I don't want any more questions. I want to go home.

We wait a long time. Grace and Abby make snowballs out of cotton balls. When they throw them, the snowballs separate and cotton balls spew over the floor. Mom and I keep looking at each other. Teddy stares at the wall.

"I wonder where everyone went," Mom says a couple of times. Teddy begins knocking on his cast with the knuckles on his other hand. It's completely hard now. I go to the door and look down the hall.

I turn back and my eyes meet Grace's. She's worried, and I feel this awful, shameful burning in my stomach. Does she believe Teddy fell down the stairs? What did she think of Dad in his bathrobe? As much as she and Carollyn helped us, if only they hadn't been there tonight!

The doctor and Carollyn return with another woman.

She sticks out her hand to Mom. "I'm Beth Harrison. I'm a social worker here at the hospital."

The smile fades from Mom's face, and I feel prickles start up my back. Something about the woman's smile— too wide, too stiff—scares me. Abby leans into my side.

"She wants to speak to each of you," Carollyn says.

"I'll speak to Teddy first, and then I'll come get the rest of you," Beth Harrison says. Carollyn leads us out the door.

In the waiting room Grace tries to talk to me, but I can't stand still. I look out the window, then down the hall. Why doesn't Beth Harrison want to talk to us together?

Teddy returns after about fifteen minutes, and then it's Mom's turn. When she returns, Abby goes. I desperately want to ask Mom what she said to Beth Harrison, but I'm afraid to bring it up in front of Carollyn and Grace.

Carollyn watches me. "It's okay, Meg. You haven't done anything wrong."

Abby's face is white when she returns. She squeezes my hand and wants to say something, but Beth Harrison pulls me out of the room. I follow her into the examining room. Before she even shuts the door, I say, "I really can't tell you anything, because I wasn't there."

"Sit down," she says, motioning to a chair. I can't look at her. "I just wanted to talk to you, see how you are. How everything is at home."

"Fine."

"I understand that your father is still at home."

I nod. I look at the different-colored plaster strips on the wall. Teddy chose blue. I think if Dad broke my arm, I'd pick pink. Bright hot pink.

"I understand you moved here in September. It must have been pretty stressful for all of you to move and start over again."

She wears a white turtleneck that hugs her throat. She's still smiling. Where is she headed? What did the others tell her? What did Abby tell her? What should I say?

"Is everything okay at home?"

I nod.

"The reason I ask is because what Teddy told us happened doesn't really match up with the injuries he has. Frankly, the doctor is very concerned."

She's still smiling. I stare at her. What will happen to us if I tell the truth?

"I know you weren't there to see what happened, so let's talk about home. Moving, dealing with everyday pressures. This can be stressful. Do your parents argue?"

"Did Abby tell you that?" *Careful.* I grip the sides of the chair. I must not tell her about Dad. If he ever found out about this . . .

"I want to hear what *you* have to say. Is your father ever aggressive or violent?"

He has never hurt me. "No." But the word burns on my lips.

"Does either of your parents abuse drugs or alcohol?"

She knows!

I grip the chair tighter. It feels as if the walls might

crash in. As if Dad will storm through the door and throw me to the ground. But the walls stay where they are. Dad is at home.

Beth Harrison stares at me, her smile fading and her eyes softer. Suddenly I'm filled with a warm, calmer feeling. And surprise. I never imagined that I'd feel anything but shame and embarrassment and fear if anyone knew about Dad.

"It's okay for you to talk," she says, her voice lower. "And it's not okay for anyone to treat you badly. It's not okay for anyone to harm you in *any* way."

If I told her about Dad, would she be able to help? But what if she called the police and they put him in jail? He'd never forgive me. Mom always says, *If only he'd stop drinking.* I feel something thick in my throat when I see Mom's face in my mind.

"I know that's not okay," I say. My hands are shaking like Mom's. I sit on them.

"How do you know that it's not okay?"

"Because I just do and because of Mom."

"What about your mom?" Beth Harrison sits perfectly still. Not even her eyes seem to blink. "Does your mom ever hurt you?"

"No, of course not! Mom is the nicest person in the world. She wouldn't hurt anyone. She's the one who holds us together."

"So you feel good about your mom."

I squeeze the bottoms of my thighs. I won't talk about Dad. But I can talk about Mom, can't I? She hasn't done anything wrong. Has she? She's the one who gets picked on, who gets blamed for everything, who Dad makes cry the most. It's not fair.

"Mom should be treated like a queen," I say. Dad should be so grateful that Mom cleaned him up and put him to bed the other night. But I frown. Maybe she should have just left him there. Taught him a lesson. I bite the cuticles on my thumb.

"Are you saying that she's not treated like a queen?"

"I don't know. No."

"What do you think that should look like, being treated like a queen?"

"Well, she should have friends and everyone should be nice to her. She shouldn't have to work so hard and not be appreciated. Her hands shouldn't shake so much."

"It sounds like you appreciate her."

"I do. She puts up with everything."

"Like what?"

I lick my lips. "I don't know. Like everything."

"Who doesn't appreciate her? Your father?"

I nod but I don't say anything.

"Why do her hands shake? Is she afraid of something?"

I drop my eyes.

Beth Harrison lowers her voice yet again. "Is she afraid of your father?"

I look at the colored plaster strips on the wall. How scared I was on the way here, that Dad would chase us and pull me from the car! I hug my arms to my chest, cold.

"Does your father hurt your mother?"

Did Abby tell her that? Beth Harrison is no longer smiling. She sits straight in her chair, her body forward, so strong and certain. I should tell her everything and she'll wrap her arms around me and tell me how brave I am and that she'll take care of me.

But she brings everything back to Dad. And I barely know her.

I see Mom's face, and I realize that it's her arms I want wrapped around me. I want *her* to tell me that she'll take care of me. But she can't do that. Was she ever able to do it? Something hot flashes in my chest, but I push it away. I don't want these feelings.

"I want my mom to be happy," I say.

Beth Harrison nods. "And she's not happy?"

I shake my head. I've said too much. I drop my eyes, and when Beth Harrison asks me why, I don't answer. We're quiet for a long time. When she asks if I want to talk more about Mom, I tell her no.

Finally she hands me her card. "Call me anytime, if you ever want to talk."

I nod, and we go back to the waiting room. Mom and Teddy watch me, their eyebrows raised, waiting. Abby chews on her nails. Grace looks as if she might cry.

"What's going on?" Grace asks me. "I don't understand what's going on."

"Nothing." I try to smile. "Everything is fine."

Beth Harrison leads all of us except Grace and Carollyn back to the exam room.

"By law I'm required to file a report to Child Protective Services when I feel that there has been some kind of abuse in a family," Beth Harrison says after she shuts the door. She motions for us to sit, but we don't. We stand lined up, close together.

She continues. "A screener will look at the report to determine if an investigation should be opened. If that happens, you'll be notified within ten days, and someone will come to the house to interview all of you."

"Interview us? All of us?" Mom asks. I know she's thinking about what Dad will say. I ball my hands into tight fists and dig them into my thighs. Abby leans into my side.

"Yes." Beth Harrison frowns and looks at us, one at a time. "But I doubt that will happen. My gut instinct tells me that someone in the family caused this injury to Teddy. But your accounts, the ones I have to write in the report, don't reflect that. And I'm afraid a screener probably won't launch an investigation based only on my instincts."

"So no one is coming to the house?" Mom asks. I can't tell if she's relieved or disappointed.

"Not unless you can tell me, now, something different," Beth Harrison says.

I stare at Mom. *Tell her,* I want to scream. *Tell her.* You have to tell her everything. *Now.* Not us. *You!*

But Mom is quiet.

"It's not okay for a family member to hurt you in any way," Beth Harrison says. "I'm not just talking about physically, but also emotionally. Name calling. Threats."

Still Mom says nothing. My heart races. Tell her!

Beth Harrison looks at Mom. "Your children are

worried about you. If your husband is harming you in any way, it's not okay. You put your family at great risk by not doing anything about it."

I glance at Mom. Her face is pale. Beth Harrison reaches into her bag and pulls out a piece of paper. She writes something and hands it to Mom.

"This is the name of a therapist. I can't tell you what to do, but I can make recommendations. I understand how difficult and frightening it may be to talk about these things. But call her. Go see her. She can help you."

Mom doesn't move. I take the paper and hand it to her.

We follow Beth Harrison back to the waiting room. Then we all walk, silently, into the cold night. I squeeze into the backseat of the car with Teddy, Grace, and Abby. It's dark and I can't see Teddy's cast, but I feel the hardness of it as it rests against my thigh. Teddy looks out the window. He's very quiet. He's very far away.

"Are you going to be okay?" Carollyn asks. We drive away.

Mom nods. "Thank you for all you've done. Teddy should heal just fine."

Carollyn glances at Mom. She isn't asking about Teddy's arm. How much does she know? After all, she left with the doctor and returned with the social worker. And Carollyn is a nurse. She knows blood vessels don't break like that when you fall.

Every light in our house is still on. Abby, Teddy, and I wait in the living room while Mom checks her bedroom. When she returns and nods, I know Dad is passed out.

"Who talked to that lady about Mom?" Teddy asks.

"I didn't say anything," Abby says. They look at me.

"But I didn't tell her about Dad." I hesitate. "All I said was that Mom puts up with everything and that it's not fair."

Mom sits on the edge of the couch. Her face is still pale and her eyes are full of tears. I've never seen her like this, so frail and tiny. I kneel in front of her. "I'm sorry."

"She said that I'm putting you at great risk by not do-ing anything," Mom says. She stares at her hands, but I keep my eyes on her face. "At great risk, she said."

"That's not true," Teddy says quickly. "This is his fault, not yours."

"But I haven't done anything to stop him."

"You can't!" Teddy says. "He's a bully. He's a drunk and a bully."

"That's not what I mean." Mom keeps shaking her head.

This is my fault. I didn't mean to get Mom in trouble. I don't want to upset her. I look at her hands. She rubs the paper Beth Harrison gave her back and forth be-tween her thumb and fingers. But I can't get these words out of my head. She's put us at *great risk.*

"You don't have to see that person." But my voice stumbles.

"He won't like it," she says slowly. "But maybe I do need to go."

I sit back on my heels. Mom's cheeks are flushed now, her lips pinched together.

Later, in our room, I pull the card out of my pocket.

Beth Harrison. MSW. Lake Haven Hospital. 555–3084.
That warm feeling I had in the hospital flows down my arms and into my fingers. She has a gut instinct about us. All we have to do is call her.

Now someone else knows. And this suddenly feels so different, maybe even *good*, that I smile, just slightly.

"What?" Abby asks. She looks down at my card. Then she opens her hand. She has an identical card, although hers is crumpled from being held so tightly in her fist all night. Still, we hold the cards side by side and stare at them.

Chapter 49

In the morning I wake just as light streams over the windowsill. Why does Dad always pick on Teddy? Maybe he doesn't love him. If he doesn't love Teddy, then maybe he doesn't love the rest of us, either. I don't know what's going to happen tomorrow or the next day. I don't know if Dad will ever stop drinking.

Before going downstairs I stare at Beth Harrison's card. Then I shove it in my desk, under paper and a ruler and an extra box of pencils.

I'm the first one up. At least, I think I am. I put my ear to Mom and Dad's closed door. Sobbing. And it's coming from Dad.

I don't hear Mom's voice. "Mom? Mom, are you in there?"

The crying quiets, and then Mom opens the door. "I'll be right out."

Over her shoulder I see Dad on the bed, in his red striped boxers, his head in his hands. When he looks up at me, his face twisted with tears and snot, I suck in my breath.

"I'm sorry, I'm sorry," he mutters. I squeeze the door with both hands. I feel the blood leave my head, and then I'm dizzy. What will happen to us if he can't go to work?

Later Dad comes to breakfast dressed in chinos and his blue work shirt. His eyes are swollen and bloodshot. My stomach is so full of nerves that I can't eat my cereal. When Teddy rests his cast on the table, Dad stares at it but doesn't say anything.

I just feel so relieved knowing he's going to work.

After school I race home and up to Teddy's room with my sketchbook. He's just as I left him that morning, lying in bed. I wonder if he's moved all day.

When Abby comes home, she brings her new bus into Teddy's room and we sit on the floor and play. We listen to that loud song Teddy likes.

When it's time for dinner we go about our chores quietly. We eat in silence. We pay no attention to Dad, although his presence feels like a splinter in my skin. When I pass him the bread, our eyes lock and I see sadness. But I turn away. Stay mad.

Later I pull my blankets and pillow into Teddy's room and make a bed on the floor. I've gotten used to not seeing his posters on the walls and his pirate ship on his bureau. But his room looks so empty.

"What happened last night?" I ask.

"You know what happened. It's the same as always. He was drunk and started calling me names. Then he grabbed me. He broke my arm."

"I should have helped. I wanted to. Then Carollyn had you in the car."

Teddy is quiet for a moment. "Everything is screwed

147

up all the time. And did you see the way that lady looked at Mom? You shouldn't have said anything about Mom, Meg. You should've kept quiet. This isn't her fault."

I know Dad's drinking isn't Mom's fault. But what was so wrong with what I said? "You heard Beth Harrison, Teddy. Mom is putting us at great risk. Look at your arm!"

"She already feels bad enough. I don't want to make it worse. I hate when she cries all the time."

I want Mom to be happy. But I can't shake this idea that it might be a good thing that someone else knows what's going on.

When I hear Mom come up the stairs, I put the blanket over my head.

"Grace is on the phone," Mom says.

I pretend I'm asleep.

"Is she asleep?"

"I don't know," Teddy says. I hear Mom leave but still I don't move. "Meg? Meg, are you asleep?" he asks.

I don't answer. Every time I saw Grace today, I wanted to run. She stopped me as we left science, asking, "How's Teddy? What did that social worker say to you? What happened when you got home? Where's your dad? *What happened?*"

"Everything's okay," I said. "Much better. It was an accident."

I must have dozed off, because the next thing I know, Abby is snuggling next to me. I sit up. Teddy is asleep.

It's ten-thirty. I go to the stairs and listen. The TV is still on.

Dad sits in his chair. The living room is dark, but he's lit up from the glow of the TV screen. He looks like a cornered animal. It freezes me on the stairs.

I dash through the living room, behind his chair, and into the kitchen. Mom sits with her elbow resting on the table and holding her head. When she sees me she seems to brighten.

"Are you okay?" I ask.

The newspaper is next to her, folded to the help wanted ads. "Today is my dad's birthday. He'd have been eighty-three."

I sit next to her and push the ashtray away.

"He never complained about anything, even after his second stroke." She sighs.

"But then you helped him learn to walk." I know this story. "It was a miracle."

Mom stubs out her cigarette. "I don't know if it was a miracle or just a lot of hard, hard work."

She gets up and we walk by Dad quickly, but he pays us no attention. Mom gets into her bed and brings her legs up to her chest. She reminds me of Abby, curled up. I close my eyes to see her when she stands tall, her eyes on the bowling pins.

Chapter 50

The robber digs up the jewels and puts dynamite in the corner. The ticker has ten minutes left on it before the whole cave blows up.

"Now what are we going to do?" Emily cries. The girls sit in the dirt, their arms tied behind them.

"Just concentrate on getting out of the ropes," Samantha says.

So the girls close their eyes and concentrate really hard. And pretty soon Samantha wiggles out of the ropes around her wrists. Then she unties Emily and they climb the rocks to the opening in the cave's ceiling.

Chapter 51

Teddy goes back to school. Aunt Jane calls, and I tell her, "We're more than halfway finished with our book. I can't wait for you to read it."

Today I see Grace rounding the corner before lunch, and I duck into the bathroom and sit in my old stall. I feel the cold creeping up my legs. After school I run to the bus.

When Abby slams the door today, Mom jumps and dumps a whole bowl of spaghetti into the sink. I'm always looking around, making sure I know where Dad is.

At dinner he tries to talk to us: How was school? What about this cold? We don't answer.

"I know what you're doing. You've made some kind of pact not to speak to me."

"Bob, we're all just trying to get by here," Mom says.

"Yeah, well, you're going to have to talk to me sometime."

Teddy's cast makes a sawing noise as he rubs it on the edge of the table. Dad opens his mouth to yell at Teddy to stop. But he snaps it closed.

Later Dad goes into the living room. Mom, Teddy, Abby, and I sit at the table.

"Did you tell him what happened at the hospital?" Teddy whispers. Mom shakes her head. "You should tell him. What if they do an investigation?"

"I'll tell him." She stares at Teddy's cast.

I don't want to be around when she does, but I can't let her do it alone. I think about what Beth Harrison said: it's not our fault. He shouldn't hurt us.

Chapter 52

Grace finds me on the way to the bus after school today. "You're ignoring me. You wouldn't talk to me in lunch today or any day since the hospital. You won't call me back. What's going on?"

"Nothing," I say. We walk down the hall and out the door.

"You're lying. That's worse! Why won't you talk to me? You tell everyone else all these things—about your grandpa in Australia and that you got a disease in some foreign country. And you won't even tell me what happened the other night."

Something sticks in my throat. I've never seen her angry like this. I walk faster.

"Aren't we best friends?" she asks.

Best friends! *Aren't we best friends?*

I stop and stare at her. All these things flash through my head: How Aunt Jane and her best friend always talk about how they feel. How Grace has told me about her mom. How much I wanted to have a best friend.

Well, here she is. But I haven't told her a *thing*. Nothing.

And she called me her best friend. Me. *Meg*.

I start walking again, my heart pounding. Part of me wants to tell her about my family, but the other part . . . Then I remember that feeling I had when Beth Harrison handed me her card. *It's okay to talk about this.*

"Your dad did that to Teddy, didn't he?" she asks softly. I nod. "Has he done stuff like that before?"

"Not like that. Before it was lots of yelling and grabbing. When he was drunk."

Once I say this, the words tumble out. About the bottles he hides in the basement, the names he calls us, how we've moved so much because he's so unhappy all the time. How hard it is now that Teddy is fighting back. I tell her about bowling and the mall.

Soon we're in front of her house. I'm dizzy from walking and talking. The whole time Grace listens and kicks the snow. Finally I stop talking.

"It's awful," she says. "But every family is messed up. In *some* way."

I smile at her. If anyone were to drive by and see us now, I bet they'd think we were just two best friends walking home from school, talking about our day.

We go inside and eat an entire box of frozen Girl Scout Thin Mints. When Carollyn comes home, she doesn't take off her coat. She hurries to hug me. "I'm so happy to see you! How is Teddy? How are you?"

Should I tell her? Grace's face is tight, as if she's fiercely keeping her mouth closed. I'm glad. Carollyn may suspect what happened, but I can't talk about it with her yet. I don't know why.

"Fine," I say.

When it's time to go, Grace stands inside the door as I walk down the steps. It's almost dark, and so cold I see my breath. Standing outside in the snow, I feel really aware of everything around me—the train whistle and the slush splashing on the curb as cars pass and the fact that I *can't* smell the foundry, even when I take a deep breath.

"Is there a national holiday in Australia named after your great-grandpa?" Grace asks.

Marty must have told her. I bite my lip. I look down the street. Mom should be here by now.

A neighbor walks by with her dog. Grace smiles and says hello. *She's so nice.* And I'm not. I'm a liar.

I see a car slow, and I start down the walk.

"Wait," Grace says.

Mom pulls up and I open the door. "I've got to go!" We drive away.

Best friends. I feel light, airy. I wiggle my toes. I smile so wide that my jaw hurts. But then I hear Grace's voice: *Is there a national holiday in Australia named after your great-grandpa?*

Chapter 53

Teddy is fifteen today. Mom takes us to two stores before Abby and I find the right present. He wants to save money to buy a car, so we find him a poster of a 1965 Mustang convertible. When he unrolls the poster after dinner, he smiles and says, "All right!" He sets it on the table next to the CDs Aunt Jane and Uncle Terry sent him.

Mom says to Dad, "Will you light the candles, Bob? Will you get forks for the cake?" Abby giggles when Dad drops a fork, leans over, and says in his best Mr. Higgins voice, "Where's that goldarn fork?"

Teddy doesn't laugh. I wonder if he's thinking about his birthday last year. Mom took him, Pete, and Harris to Fun and Games, the video arcade. It's been a long time since I've heard Teddy talk about friends.

Teddy puts his cast on the table, and with his other hand he pulls on the hairs on his chin. He'd be angry if he knew I told Grace about Dad. Teddy always says that nothing good comes from telling anyone. I wish I could tell him how relieved I feel. I wish he could feel this way, too.

The next day is cleaning day. Grace acts completely normal and says nothing about our conversation the other day.

We flip a coin to see who will clean the bathroom. Grace loses. She plops down on the couch and sulks. "It's so disgusting sticking your hand in the toilet." She shivers. "Double or nothing?" When I say no, she brings her legs up and sits cross-legged.

I glance at the clock. I have math and reading to do after we finish, and I have to be home before dinner. I could offer to clean the bathroom, but I've done it the past two weeks in a row. I shift my feet and stare at her. She stares back.

I walk into the supply cabinet and bring back a pair of latex gloves. I toss them to Grace. "Here, now you don't have to worry about your hands."

She giggles. "Come here." In the bathroom she holds the open end of the glove under the faucet. Water pours into the fingers, swelling them like sausages. Then she ties the open end closed. She tosses it at me. We laugh as we throw the bloated hand back and forth.

"Go long!" Grace yells. The hand brushes the ceiling, but still I catch it. The knot loosens, and I try to tighten it. "Just throw it. It won't come undone."

I throw the hand the length of the room. Just as Grace catches it, water explodes down the front of her. We laugh so hard that neither of us can talk.

Finally I say, "Serves you right."

She cleans the bathroom, although I've finished with everything else by the time she's through. Then we eat the rest of the going-away cake Dr. Bennett brought in for

Kathy, his receptionist, who is going on maternity leave. We spread our homework on the floor. I should do math, but instead I open my book about Eleanor Roosevelt.

Her father was an alcoholic. Both her parents died before she was ten, and she went to live with her strict old grandma. Eleanor used to hide books under her mattress and read at night because her grandma wanted her to read only at certain times of the day.

I read a passage to Grace. "So this writer is saying that the bad stuff that happened in Eleanor's life made her sympathetic to people because she believed that all humans have 'failings'?"

"I get that, don't you?" Grace asks. "Like, it's hard to be understanding of people unless you've been through something really bad yourself."

"You can be understanding all you want, but what if someone does something really bad?" I want to stay angry at Dad.

Grace sits up. "It feels just awful being mad at people. Don't you think?"

But there are different kinds of being mad at people. I get irritated when Grace tries to get out of cleaning. But it's a lot different from how mad I am at Dad.

Then I remember what Grace's great-aunt Melinda said. *Grace was so angry.* She was angry at those people who lied to her when her mom was sick. So maybe feeling angry at people hurts too much because it reminds her of her mom.

At least I stopped lying to her about my family.

Chapter 54

We wait for Dad in the kitchen. Abby stands at the door and looks through the curtain. Teddy drums the fingers of his other hand on his cast.

"Why tonight?" Teddy asks. "No one's called about an investigation."

"I don't think anyone will call," Mom says. "But this is a good time. He's not drinking. He should know."

She whirls away from the stove. Something's different.

When Dad gets home, we all sit down to eat. Mom has made Dad's favorite dinner. He cuts his meat loaf in thick pieces and eats fast, as if he's afraid it will get cold. He's happy. He's going flying after dinner.

"The other night at the hospital we told the doctor that Teddy fell down the stairs." Mom's words are quick. I set down my fork. "But she noticed bruises across Teddy's arm. You don't get bruises from falling down stairs, she said. You get them from being grabbed."

Dad stops chewing and shifts his food into his cheek. "Yeah, so?"

"Well, then a social worker came to talk to us and said that she was filing a report with Child Protective Services. The doctor is worried because what we told her doesn't match Teddy's injuries. They might do an investigation."

Dad pushes away from the table. "What did you tell them?"

"Nothing, Bob." Mom's voice jumps, and I suck in my breath. "We didn't say anything. We didn't have to. This is all because of the bruises. Now I guess we wait."

"Wait? Oh, Christ."

Mom has him. She's done it. There's nothing he can say.

"Why didn't you tell me this sooner? Why did you wait until now?"

"I didn't think they'd actually do an investigation. But I got a call today from Child Protective Services. They're requiring me to go to a therapist. They didn't say this, but I got the feeling that if I go, they won't do an investigation."

"You? Why do you have to do anything?"

Mom grips the sides of her pants. "You'd rather they start an investigation?"

Dad slams his hand on the table, and we jump. He gets up and starts for the basement, then turns. "You aren't to be blabbing with everyone."

He stomps down the stairs. Mom slides down in her chair.

"Somebody called?" Abby asks.

"No. But I made an appointment with the therapist. I had to tell him something."

How easy it is for us to lie! How hard it is to tell the truth!

Teddy shakes his head. "It's going to end up bad, Ma. Everything is always bad."

"What's done is done."

"Maybe it's okay," I say. "Maybe this will scare him and he'll stop drinking."

"He'll take it out on us," Teddy says.

"No harm letting him worry." Mom stares at me, her eyebrows raised. "That's what Shawna says. Let the man *stew* for a while."

"You talked to her about Dad?" Teddy asks.

Mom shakes her head. "Just listened to her talk about her ex-husband."

I nod. What if Mom tells that therapist everything? I tip back in my chair.

But when I hear Dad's boots on the stairs, I bring my chair down hard on the floor.

Chapter 55

"What are you talking about?" Roxanne asks. She and Ariel put their lunch trays on the table at the same time and sit.

"Meg is writing a book," Grace says. We'd been talking about how Emily and Samantha escape from the cave.

"What's it about?" Ariel leans toward me.

"Two girls who solve crimes," I say. "And Grace is drawing pictures for it."

"How do you know how to write a book?" Roxanne opens her Jell-O.

Grace and I look at each other and shrug. Ideas just come to us. Ariel sits back, smiling.

"What?" I ask.

"Wow!" Ariel says. "You're a great writer. And Grace is a great artist. What a cool, cool idea."

"Thanks!"

"Where do you get the stuff to write about?" Roxanne asks. "You make it up?"

"Meg has a very *vivid* imagination," Grace says. That's what Carollyn said to me the other night after she read part of our book.

"Who's going to be your editor?" Ariel says. "Me!"

I start nodding and so does Grace.

"Wow," Roxanne says as she squeezes her Jell-O out of the container and onto her peas. Then she pokes at it, making it wobble. "You guys are going to be famous. I can just tell."

And Grace and I burst out laughing.

The next night Dr. Bennett and I pop popcorn. There's a fire in the fireplace, and Ricky has the movie ready. Grace is getting blankets. There's no place I'd rather be.

"How's Teddy's arm?" Dr. Bennett asks.

I pour Pepsi into plastic cups. When I glance up, he's looking at me. And this shoots out of my mouth: "My dad is an alcoholic."

I've never said that word out loud. But that's what Dad is. I feel a little tingle start up my back.

"Well, Meggers, so is my dad," Dr. Bennett says. "He drank for twenty years before he stopped. But by that time the damage was done."

"What do you mean?"

"You can't drink for that long and not put your family through a lot of pain. It took a long time for me to get my act together. I'm *still* working at it."

I want to ask what *get my act together* means. But then Ricky tells us the movie is ready.

In the morning I wake before the sun comes up. Grace isn't in her sleeping bag. When she doesn't come back, I

163

go look for her. No one else is awake. I find her on the floor in front of the TV. I sit next to her, but she doesn't look at me, that's how hard she's concentrating on the screen.

She watches a pretty blond woman feed a baby in a highchair. The woman keeps giggling and turning to the camera. The camera zooms in for a close-up. The woman has lots of freckles and blue eyes and the kind of open face that Carollyn has. You want her to wrap her arms around you, because you can trust a person with a face like that.

I hear Dr. Bennett's voice on TV, and I realize he was making the video. The face on the screen is Grace's mom, and the baby must be Grace. After that the TV screen goes blank.

"I woke up this morning," Grace says, "and I couldn't remember what my mom looked like. This has been happening to me a lot. I couldn't remember. It scares me so much. I'd give anything to have her back. Just to talk to her. Even for one day."

I don't know what to say, but I feel as if my heart is breaking. "Do you want to watch the video again?"

She nods. So I rewind the tape and we watch it in silence, over and over again, until the sun peeks up over the windowsill.

Chapter 56

Yesterday Mom went to see the therapist and came home with red eyes. The only thing she told us was that the therapist will charge Mom only half of what she normally charges. Then Mom went to her room and shut the door. Teddy and I think it didn't go well.

In study hall I stare at the bookshelves until my eyes blur. Beth Harrison said she had a gut instinct about us. If Mom told that therapist what happened to Teddy, another person knows.

Teddy got a job at the gas station near our house.

Today after my newspaper meeting, I walk there. I stand next to the pump and watch Teddy through the window. His hair is tucked behind his ears, and he wears a dark blue button-down shirt that hangs to his thighs.

He holds a cigarette and flicks the ashes. Something about the way he does this looks both familiar and far away. My stomach turns, and not just because I hate cigarette smoke. I can't stop thinking, *Teddy has kept it a secret from me.*

He stuffs the cigarette into the ashtray when I walk in the door.

"What are you doing here?" He glances at another guy. They laugh.

"What's so funny?"

Teddy shrugs. Why is he so rude? He's never acted like this. I glance at the guy. He has a ponytail that goes halfway down his back. His hands are black with grease.

Teddy takes off the shirt and hangs it next to the door. "Catch you later," he says to the guy. He walks two steps ahead of me.

"Why are you smoking?" I ask once we're on the sidewalk.

Teddy waits for me. As we start walking, his cast bumps against me. "I don't really do it that much."

It's warm for March, and the snow has begun to melt. I'd been feeling pretty good because I figured this could be the last snow of the year. But then the wind whips around the corner, and the cold goes right through me. I feel like crying, but I don't know why.

I've kept secrets from Teddy, too. I've written a book. I've wished that I lived at Grace's. And I talked about Dad with Grace and Dr. Bennett, and I *liked* it.

"Do you think things could be different now?" I ask. "Because of the hospital and the therapist?"

"Dad won't stop drinking because Mom's talking to someone."

I kick a clump of snow, and it breaks into a hundred pieces. I zip my coat to my neck. He's right. But I've been feeling so different—a bit hopeful—the last couple of days.

"Yeah, but no one has ever really known before, at least not outside our family."

Something has to change. I feel it. But if Dad won't stop drinking, what is it?

And I wonder, for the first time, if maybe we're the ones who have to change.

Chapter 57

"How's your dad?" Dr. Bennett asks.

Something in his voice, a sharpness that isn't usually there, makes me lift my head and look at him. He's cutting onions at the counter, but he's looking at me. I fold my arms across my chest. I glance at Carollyn washing lettuce in the sink.

"Okay." Why do I say this?

"It's a tricky disease. I'm sure you wish you could help him. But there's not much you can do, Meg. Only he can decide to stop drinking."

There's not much you can do.

I've always believed that we need to help him. But maybe Dr. Bennett is right.

At dinner the Bennetts tell me about a house they rent every year on Lake Michigan. Last year, Grace says, her dad climbed up into the dropped ceiling and hid. When they came into the room, he said, "This is God talking." No one could figure out where the voice was coming from until Dr. Bennett crashed out of the ceiling and fell to the floor.

Grace and Ricky laugh so hard they can't talk. I make myself smile.

Carollyn watches me. She knows what really happened to Teddy. Would she tell? When she catches me looking at her, she tilts her head and smiles. I squirm in my seat. Should I go home?

I blurt out, "My dad made this discovery that saved the foundry tons of money. He got a big bonus. We're going to Disney World."

"That's great." But Carollyn's head is still tilted. *This is the truth*, I want to say.

"Are things better now?" Dr. Bennett is frowning.

"Everything's fine." It hurts to look at him. So I ask him to tell me more about the house on Lake Michigan.

Later, as Carollyn drives me home, she keeps glancing at me. When she pulls into our driveway, she says, "Meg . . ." I thank her and jump out.

Inside our kitchen I stare at the dishes stacked on the counter. I don't want to be here, either. But where am I supposed to go?

Chapter 58

The Great Faces presentations start this week. Marty dresses up like Albert Einstein, with a crazy wig and a fake mustache.

"You were great," I tell him in the newspaper room after school. He and Grace are at the computer, trying to rewrite a headline for Marty's editorial on our awful school lunches.

"Thanks," he says. "When do you go?"

"After spring break."

"I still wish you were doing your great-grandpa."

"Doing what about her great-grandpa?" Grace asks.

Marty turns to Grace. "Her great-grandpa would've made an awesome Great Face. Hey, you could've reenacted him killing that shark. That would've been so cool."

"What shark?" Grace turns to me. "What are you talking about?"

I should tell her. I should tell both of them that I made it up.

Marty keeps staring at me, and I try to smile, but I feel my bottom lip start to quiver. Marty wrinkles up his forehead.

"I've been thinking about this. Did he kill the shark with a spear? I mean, I don't think it's so easy to kill a shark. Right? He must have gone out in a boat. You can't do it from shore. But I guess you could shoot it from the shore. So how did he do it?"

If I tell them the truth, then I won't have to worry about Grace finding out that I've told all these lies. But how do I explain why I lied?

"Is this about that great-grandpa in Australia?" Grace asks.

"It's not a big deal." I jerk my head around. Mrs. Hollis stands in the doorway, looking at a notebook. "Oh! I need to ask Mrs. Hollis something."

I hurry out past Mrs. Hollis and don't stop until I push open the door to the girls' bathroom. I sit in my old stall. With my finger I trace the names etched in the metal. Jennifer. Joey. Roxanne.

Having Grace for a friend is the best thing that has ever happened to me. Why can't I tell her the whole truth about anything?

Chapter 59

"Who left the outside lights on? Who left the towels on the bathroom floor? There's no ketchup. Why can't anyone put things back where they belong?" Dad barks from the kitchen.

We're in the living room. It's the start of our spring break, and we get to stay up late to watch a movie.

"Let's get out of here." Mom stands, and we follow her into the kitchen and put on our coats.

"Where are you going?" Dad asks.

Mom holds the door open. "It's none of your business. Come on, kids."

"It is my business," Dad says. "I'll make you stay."

"You lay a hand on me and I'll call Child Protective Services." Mom glares at him. Then we're out the door.

"Are we going bowling?" Abby asks once we're in the car.

"Yes."

"Would you really call someone on Dad?" Teddy opens the window just a crack.

"I don't know. I don't know anything anymore."

"It would just make him mad," Teddy says.

"So what?" This pops out before I think. They turn and look at me.

"You want to see him go crazy on Mom if she calls that lady?" Teddy points at me. "You want to live with him like *that*?"

"Why do we have to live with him at all?" something makes me say.

Teddy looks at me and then Mom. "Yeah, Ma. Why not? Let's leave him."

"How would we live? On what? I can't find a job. Shawna at least has a degree. Which is more than I have. It costs money to be on your own. Where would we go?"

"How does Shawna do it?" I lean forward.

"She gets money from her ex-husband. And she has a job at an insurance agency."

Now that I've said it out loud, I can't get it out of my mind. Yes, let's leave him. We can do this!

Teddy and Mom feel it, too. They keep turning and looking at each other, then at me. And there's something in Mom's eyes that I haven't seen before.

At the bowling alley Mom charges in the door. We hurry to keep up with her. We find our lane, and Mom is the first to change her shoes and find a ball. She stands at the top of the lane, eyes the pins, and then slides her knee to the floor and lets go. The ball shoots out of her hand and crashes into the pins so hard it hurts to hear it.

"What if you break the pins?" Abby asks when Mom sits.

"My dad's ball was a lot faster than mine, and nothing ever broke."

When it's Teddy's turn, he only gets three pins.

Mom likes bowling because she's good at it and because it reminds her of her dad. I wonder if I'll have any good memories of my dad. "Why is Dad so unhappy?"

Abby stands at the top of the lane, her ball on the floor. "Help!" She giggles and Teddy jumps up. They count to three and push the ball. It wobbles down the lane.

"He's upset with his boss. You know how he is."

"Yeah, but I mean, he's always been unhappy, Mom, even as a kid, I bet."

I think of those pictures of Dad and how Aunt Jane said that he took the brunt of things, and I think of Dr. Bennett's comments about how his dad's drinking messed up their family.

"When life gives you lemons, you make lemonade." Mom's voice shakes and she won't look at me. "It's your turn. Bend your knees. And remember to stay low."

I stand. I bend my right knee and stay low and let the ball go. I glare at it, willing it down the lane. When my ball takes out all but one pin, I yell, "Yes!"

Teddy looks at the scorecard. "Better watch out, Mom. Meg's in the lead."

Chapter 60

On Wednesday it's unusually warm. When Aunt Jane calls this morning, I tell her that the temperature is 65 degrees.

"You lucky!" she says. "It's supposed to snow in Boston."

"Too bad you don't live here."

After I hang up, Abby comes into the kitchen wearing shorts and pink flip-flops. We bake cookies and decide to take them to Teddy at work. Two streets over a woman rakes her yard. When her dog waddles over to us, Abby bends down and he licks her face.

"Oh, he's so cute." Abby wraps her arms around his neck and kisses him.

"You're an animal lover," the woman says. I've seen her before, and then I remember. She was one of the Welcome Wagon women. "Let me show you something."

We follow her into the garage. A black cat and four kittens rest on blankets in the corner. An electric space heater makes the garage warm and cozy. The kittens are all black except one, who has white around his chin.

"That's St. Nick," the woman tells us. "I haven't named the others."

"Are you keeping them?" Abby doesn't wait for an answer. "Can I have one?"

The woman laughs. "You'll have to ask your folks first. Then come see me. I'm Mrs. Miller."

Dad hates pets.

"I want a kitty," Abby says as we walk home. "Natalie is so bossy about Marshmallow. If we get a kitty, I'm not going to be bossy. I'll let Natalie hold it."

And this is all we talk about for the next two days.

Chapter 61

On Friday morning I stand in my pajamas and watch Dad's truck until it disappears. He's off to Michigan for the day on business. He wouldn't tell us anything about it. But he must be happy about the trip because for the past two days he hasn't complained about his boss. He didn't even get angry last night when Abby asked again, "Please, please, *please* can we get a kitty?"

Dad bent over and looked under the table. "Here, kitty. Where's that goldarn kitty-cat?"

Teddy makes pancakes. When it's time to turn them, he flips one in the air and tries to catch it on the spatula. He misses and it falls to the floor. If Dad were here, he'd yell. Mom just laughs, and so do we. We can laugh all day if we want.

Later Teddy, Abby, and I walk to Mrs. Miller's house. The sky is gray and cold rain falls around us. Mrs. Miller puts on her coat when we ring her bell and then takes us into the garage. Teddy bends down to look at the kittens. Abby leans on his back.

"See, there, that one," Abby says in his ear. "That's St. Nick."

We thank Mrs. Miller and leave. Out on the sidewalk

I can't stand it anymore. "What did you think? Aren't they so cute? Don't you want one?"

Teddy smiles. "Tonight when I get home from work, we'll come up with a plan."

Abby jumps up and down and squeals.

But that night when Teddy comes home, Abby and I are outside Mom and Dad's bedroom door, trying to listen. They've been in there for an hour, ever since Dad got home from Michigan. I think Mom is crying.

"Drunk?" Teddy puts his ear to the door.

When we hear their voices grow louder, we back up into the living room. Dad comes out first. Mom's eyes are red and she won't look at us. Abby reaches for my hand.

Dad starts talking. I feel my mind leave my body, and the words he says float past me. I'm on the ceiling. I'm upside down. Everything is jumbled.

"We're moving. I'm fed up. Kalamazoo is only two hours away."

Then my mind and body snap back together, and I start screaming. I run around the living room. I knock over a lamp. I trip on the leg of the couch. I want these words to go away. They follow me. Run!

"Meg!" Dad tries to catch me, but I'm too quick. I'm still screaming. Then I turn, smack into Mom, and fall. I burst into tears.

Teddy bends over. "Are you okay?"

"Leave me alone!"

"This is a good opportunity for us," Dad says. "I'm getting screwed here."

"You're always getting screwed." Mom goes into the

kitchen and returns with an ice pack. She holds it to my forehead. But I grab it and stand so quickly that Mom stumbles. I don't care. Fall down. Leave me alone.

How could you just let him take us away?

I run up the stairs. I slam my door and grab my sketchbook. Across an entire page I write *I hate Dad.* I sit against the wall and put the ice pack to my head. The cold is shocking, but then a numbness creeps over me. Cold seeps down into my body.

Later, when Mom comes upstairs, I pretend I'm asleep. I sense her hesitating over me, but I don't move. I feel her hand brush my hair off my face, and then she's gone.

Chapter 62

"We're moving to Michigan." I say this to Grace as we walk to Dr. Bennett's office. I've waited all day for the right time to tell her. But I still feel sick to my stomach.

She stops, her shoulders sinking. "You're *serious?*"

"My dad took a new job. We're moving in a couple months."

Grace's face reddens. Her nostrils flare and her whole body tenses. I think she's about to scream, but instead she bursts out crying. The sobs seem to rise up out of her chest, and her whole body shakes. "You can't leave. You can't!"

We hug and then walk as she keeps wiping her eyes. I can't even cry anymore.

Dr. Bennett is at his office when we arrive.

"Meg's moving to Michigan!" Grace blurts out before we're through the door. I tell him about my dad's new job. Dr. Bennett listens and says how sorry he is. Later he comes into the waiting room while we're dusting and sits on the couch. Then he tells us a story.

He was twelve and living in North Carolina when a big hurricane headed for his town. People boarded up buildings and moved boats from the harbor. Dr. Bennett told his parents they should move their sailboat, which was anchored in the cove near the harbor. It wasn't a big sailboat—just a little Sunfish—but he loved it more than anything.

Dr. Bennett's parents were having a party that night, and his father had already started drinking. By afternoon the sky was dark and the wind had picked up, and Dr. Bennett went to his father again. He was stinking, blind drunk.

So Dr. Bennett rode his bike down to the cove. Everyone at the marina was too busy to help him. They told him to go home.

Dr. Bennett wouldn't leave his sailboat. The wind would surely smash it if he left it there or tied it on the shore. So he came up with a plan. He swam to his boat, climbed in, and pulled the plug. The boat sank to the bottom of the cove. Then he went home.

The hurricane destroyed many homes. The boats that had been tied on the shore smashed against one another. He even saw a boat like his on the marina roof. But his boat was safe at the bottom of the cove. Later he got the Coast Guard to pull it up.

Dr. Bennett finishes and turns back to his office. Grace looks confused, but I know the point of the story. It's just like what Aunt Jane said to me that day at the airport in Boston. *You have to choose your own destiny.*

So Grace and I come up with a plan.

"You can't move," she says. "You have to stay and live with us. You *have* to."

This is my destiny, I think. If Mom won't leave Dad, then I'll move in with Grace. I won't have to worry if Dad is drinking or if he and Teddy are fighting. Dr. Bennett helped himself. That's what I'm going to do.

Chapter 63

The rocks on the cave walls are slippery and wet, but finally the girls reach the top. Emily climbs out first and then reaches her hand down to help Samantha. But Samantha loses her footing and starts to fall. Emily grabs on to her arm just in the nick of time and pulls her out.

They stand in the wavy golden dune grass and catch their breath.

"That was a close one," Samantha gasps.

Chapter 64

Bulldozers have begun ripping up part of one side of the cornfield. I'm not sure how many houses they'll build. Yesterday I counted six holes. The banging and the ding-ing from the trucks starts early. I barely hear Aunt Jane when she calls this morning.

"I can't believe you're moving again," she says. "Are you okay?"

She's worried, but pretending not to be. I straighten and grip the phone. "Yeah."

"Oh, Meg, I'm so sorry. And sorry for Grace, too."

I can't talk, because if I do I'll start crying.

"I'm sorry I haven't called. We've been so busy getting ready for the move. But I have a conference in Ann Arbor in a couple of weeks, and we want to stop and see you. One last time before Hong Kong."

A huge dump truck rumbles down the street. I don't know what to say except, "Okay, but I have to go. I have to give my report today."

"That's right! Good luck. Call me and tell me how it goes. Are you okay?"

What would it feel like to tell her the truth? "Yeah, I'm fine."

Later I sit in class and stare out the window. I don't know how it would ever work, living with Grace or all of us leaving Dad.

Just before it's my turn to give my report, I walk in slow motion to the bathroom. I change my clothes and stare in the mirror. I wear a big coat and an old-fashioned hat and pair of shoes Mom found for me. But I don't look like Eleanor Roosevelt. I don't look like me, either.

My legs wobble as I stand in front of the class. Images flash through my mind—how pathetic Dad looked in that cigarette mess, the clomping of his boots on the stairs.

Then I have these other thoughts, and they give me such a stab in my heart that I grab on to Mr. Holcomb's desk. Sweat breaks out on my neck.

Dad isn't going to stop drinking. And we'll never, ever leave him. I've been telling the biggest tall tale of my life to myself.

Grace has so many stories about her family. The only thing I *really know* about mine is that we'll move to Michigan and then we'll move someplace else and then someplace after that. Dad will never be happy, and he'll never stop drinking, and he'll never find a job he likes. Because he hates everything. And everybody.

I stare at the globe in the back of the room until my eyes blur. I feel the blood leave my head. Sweat runs down the middle of my back and across my forehead.

I have Grace and our plan. But I'm tired of thinking. I lower my eyes and read my report. I don't tell any of the stories I'd planned to use. I don't talk in the New York accent I'd rehearsed.

When I'm done, I go back to the bathroom and sit in my stall. When the bell rings, I stuff my outfit in my bag and go to social studies. I sit looking out the window.

I've always wanted to believe that life would be better, normal, because I was afraid of what it would feel like not to have any hope. Now I don't care what happens. I feel like I let the air inside me out and I'm just flat.

Chapter 65

Grace and I stand next to each other in the Bennetts' kitchen. We changed into shorts after school, and our pale bare legs look like matching toothpicks underneath us.

"Meg can live with us during the school year, and on holidays and vacations she can go back to her family," Grace tells her dad and Carollyn. "Oh, please say yes. We'll *die* if we're separated." Grace takes a deep breath and holds it.

Dr. Bennett and Carollyn look at each other. He frowns. Why aren't they as excited about this as we are?

"We don't want to see you go, Meg," Dr. Bennett says. "And we'd love to have you stay with us. But won't you miss your family?"

I look down at my bare feet.

"Is your dad drinking again?"

I shake my head. We're quiet.

"Meg," Carollyn says. "What happened that night? Tell us."

I close my eyes until I see white streaks across the black. If I tell them, will they call Beth Harrison? Will she be angry that I lied to her? Will the police do something to Dad? I want to tell. I want the Bennetts to hug me and tell me they'll help.

"Did your dad hurt Teddy?" Dr. Bennet asks.

I nod but don't look up.

"It's not okay for him to hurt Teddy," Carollyn says softly. "Or any of you."

"I know," I say, opening my eyes. "I know. Beth Harrison told us that he shouldn't ever hurt us. And she told us that if we needed her, we should call her."

Dr. Bennett and Carollyn look at each other.

There's no turning back now. "I don't want to move. This will just happen all over again. And then what?"

"You have options," Carollyn says. "Your family can leave him. Your mother can get a restraining order from the police to keep him away. And you can all stay here until you figure this out."

"We couldn't do that." What would Teddy say? What if Dad looks for us? I'd be too embarrassed. I try to picture Beth Harrison's face in my mind, but I can't. Tears sting my eyes.

Dr. Bennett and Carollyn glance at each other.

"We're going to find a way to help you," Dr. Bennett says.

People know. They want to help, not run away from us. And Dad shouldn't ever hurt us. *Ever*. I shake my hair out of my eyes and stand up. "Okay."

Grace and I go upstairs. We sit on her bed, and I watch her draw. This is one of my favorite things to do with Grace, watch how easily her hand goes across the paper. How good she is at making something out of nothing.

After a while Dr. Bennett sticks his head in Grace's room and says to me, "You told me your mom worked in a doctor's office before. Do you think she'd help me out? You know my receptionist, Kathy. She's out until mid-July on maternity leave."

"I'll ask her!"

Grace and I look at each other and raise our eyebrows at the same time. This kind of help never occurred to me. Mom could do this. She could.

I walk home. Half of the cornfield has been bulldozed. Last summer the corn grew so high you couldn't see over it. But now the stalks are just little brown and green blips across the acres.

Abby is playing hopscotch in the driveway with Natalie. The concrete is still warm. I sit and let the heat soak into my legs. Abby balances herself against Dad's truck and tosses the stone.

Teddy walks up the street. When he reaches us, he sits, smelling like cigarette smoke. Abby hops to number six.

"You know Dad's going to Michigan tomorrow to find a place," he says.

I squeeze my eyes shut and try to imagine a new house, a new street, a new town.

I open my eyes. Mom is across the street with Shawna. I hear Shawna's booming voice, but I can't make out the words. Then Mom laughs. Not since Ohio have I seen Mom so friendly with a neighbor.

Mom walks back across the street and says, "Let's go get one of the kittens."

"What about Dad?" Teddy stands.

"Oh, tough beans," Mom says.

Walking back from Mrs. Miller's, Mom carries St. Nick inside her sweater. Abby keeps petting his little head. When Mom and I look at each other, I say, "Dr. Bennett wants you to call him. His receptionist is staying home with her baby for a couple of months, and he needs someone to take her job."

At first her face doesn't move. But then she nods.

Chapter 66

When we get home, I notice how tulips have popped up across the front of the house. In the backyard more tulips line the grass just before the cornfield. I walk around, St. Nick in my arms, and show him all this new life. The only good thing about moving around as much as we do is that you never know what the different seasons will bring.

Abby takes charge of St. Nick. She makes toys out of yarn and old socks, makes a litter box and a bed, and fills bowls with food and water.

At dinner Dad tells us that he's taken a supervisor's job at a foundry in Kalamazoo. The foundry makes pilings for skyscrapers. He wants another supervisor job? All we hear is how soft management people are.

"Why do you think you'll be any happier up there than here?" Mom asks.

"Happy?" He picks up his glasses, wipes them on his shirt, and puts them on. Then he takes them off, wipes them again, looks through them, and frowns. Finally he tosses them on the table.

"Yes, happy. Isn't it always the same?"

"Fine. Then don't come with me."

"Maybe we won't." Mom is very still, her eyes fixed on Dad.

"Is this the crap that therapist is giving you? Is she telling you to do this? Or is it that busybody across the street?"

"No one is telling me to do anything." Mom's voice is steady. Dad heads toward the basement door and turns.

"You'll see how hard it is. You won't be able to leave me."

Then he slams the door and heads down the stairs. I feel my mouth fall open. But when I turn to Mom, I shut it. She's staring at her hands. *Please don't give up.*

"I don't know if I can do this," she says. Teddy puts his hand on top of hers.

"You just did," I say.

"That's because what we told him about the hospital is fresh in his mind." She pulls her hands from under Teddy's and rubs her eyes. Her shoulders are still. She's not crying. She's not shaking.

"Call Dr. Bennett," I say. "It's a job, Mom. You could make some money."

She slowly nods. I nod back, our heads in rhythm.

Chapter 67

"Let's go look at the new houses," Uncle Terry says to me.

Mom put us in charge of the grill, but it's going to be a while until the coals are ready. Mom, Aunt Jane, and Abby are shucking corn on the back stoop. Teddy is in his room with the door closed. Dad isn't home from work yet.

"Okay." I lead Uncle Terry through the cornfield. The stalks are only ankle high, and we easily step over them until we're next to the new houses. All six holes are covered with wood framing. But they're only skeletons, and it's hard to imagine what the houses will eventually look like.

"Wow," Uncle Terry says. "When you moved in, this was all cornfield. It's amazing how quickly things change."

I nod. When Dad came back from Kalamazoo two weeks ago, he said he'd found a house. No one asked about it. But now I wonder what it's like. Is it new?

We walk up close to a house. Uncle Terry grunts loudly as he pushes on a wooden stud. I giggle, and then he turns and laughs, too.

"Oh, Meg, I wish you didn't have to move again."

I look away.

He sighs. "Your mom told me she has a job."

"Yeah." She's been working for Grace's dad for almost two weeks now. She also sees the therapist twice a week, but I don't tell Uncle Terry.

"And Teddy. Think he'll come out of his room tonight?" He chuckles.

I smile and walk toward the next house. I know where Uncle Terry is headed. Pretty soon he'll run out of people to ask about, and then it will be Dad's turn. Things don't turn out well when Uncle Terry knows what's going on at home.

We walk to the end of the construction and stop.

"I thought about you when we were in Ann Arbor yesterday." He turns to me. "After Jane spoke, we walked around, looking at the dorms where we lived and the places we used to go. It's such a great school. You're plenty smart enough to go there someday. Do you ever think about college?"

No. I can't even decide where I'm going to live next year.

"Think about it. I wish I'd had someone tell me that when I was your age, Meg. I wish there was something we could do to help."

"But you're moving to Hong Kong."

"I know." He stares out over the field. "I've got an old laptop that I want to give you. You can e-mail us."

A computer! "Thank you."

I'll teach Abby how to use it. But I'll need the Internet

194

to use e-mail, and Dad calls the Internet "the big black hole."

"I don't think Dad will let us be on the Internet."

"I'll talk to him." Uncle Terry smiles, and I smile back. I change the subject.

"Why didn't my dad go to college?"

Uncle Terry runs his fingers through his hair. "Have you asked him about this?"

"He won't talk about when he grew up."

"We didn't have such an easy time. Our dad, Poppy, was a workaholic and an alcoholic. Let's just say that your dad had to put up with a lot. He was fourteen when Poppy died, and your grandma expected a lot from him. She sent him to boarding school and wanted him to take over the family business. Your dad wanted no part of it."

"Poppy was an alcoholic?"

"A mean, violent alcoholic. I don't remember a lot. I was only ten when he died. But I remember once watching Poppy drag your dad by the hair across the kitchen floor."

Skinned knees. Messy hair. Scowl.

"But wouldn't that make someone want to grow up and never drink?"

He studies me. "It takes a lot of work to get over these things that happen when you're a kid. Sometimes it's easier not to deal with any of it."

"How come you turned out okay?"

"I talk about this with Jane. It helps me to understand. But I'm still trying to sort through it. I'm just thankful that I'm not an alcoholic like Poppy. Or maybe your dad."

My cheeks burn. I keep my lips tight.

"I've always worried about him," Uncle Terry says.

I chew on the cuticle on my thumb. When I taste something tinny, I look at the blood on my thumb and wipe it on my jeans. Uncle Terry can worry and suspect all he wants, but there's no way he can be sure unless I tell him.

"Everything is pretty much okay."

"It's all right, Meg. You don't have to say anything."

I pick up a handful of dirt and let it sift through my fingers. When I look up, Uncle Terry is staring at me.

"I think a lot about a day when I was your age. I'd failed a science test. I'd never cared about school—your dad was so much smarter. But this big red F really bothered me. It was the first time I felt like I had a choice in what happened to me. I hadn't studied. I got an F. No one was going to help me except me.

"I made a deal with my teacher. I promised that if I could take the test over, I'd get an A. If I didn't, he could fail me for the semester. I was lucky he liked to bet! It was a lot of work but I got that A."

I nod. We walk back toward our house. Teddy is in the backyard, watching us.

Uncle Terry's story reminds me of the one Dr. Bennett told about his sailboat. Uncle Terry is trying to tell me that I can choose my own destiny.

Later we have dinner and laugh, and then roast marshmallows over the dying coals. It's fun, but I can't stop thinking: Poppy was an alcoholic. Dad is an alcoholic. What does this mean for us?

By the next morning my mind is a jumble when we all walk outside to say goodbye.

Dad and Uncle Terry punch each other in the arm, and then Uncle Terry grabs Dad and hugs him. Aunt Jane hugs everyone. I'm last. "I don't know when we'll see you again," I say.

I bury my face in her coat. She tightens her arms around me. I wish I were going with them. I wish . . . I wish they were my parents!

"Hong Kong suddenly seems too far away," she whispers, her voice cracking.

Tears fill my eyes, but I hold them back. I don't want her to worry. I want her to think I'm brave. I pull away. "Good luck!"

That night Abby crawls into bed next to me. I twist my finger around the hair at her temple. Her blond hair is soft and thin, just a smidge darker than Mom's.

Maybe there's not much we can do about what we get from our parents. Look at George Martins and the terrible muscle disease he got from his dad. Dad is an alcoholic like Poppy. And I got my smarts from Dad. Maybe we don't choose our destiny after all. Maybe it chooses us.

Chapter 68

The next morning I balance on the side of the tub and watch Teddy shave. He wears jeans and no shirt, and I notice how solid his shoulder muscles look. Pretty soon his hair will be down to his shoulders.

"If you have to sit there watching, at least help out." He points to a towel. When I hand it to him, I brush against his cast. Only a few more weeks until it's off.

"When Uncle Terry and I went to look at the new houses last night, I didn't say anything about Dad."

"I don't care about Dad." Something in his voice has changed, and it's not only that it's deeper.

"I told Grace about Dad." I want to tell him how nice it is to talk with someone else.

"Whatever."

After dinner Teddy shuts his door. "I want to be alone." Maybe he doesn't care about Dad. But I don't want him to stop caring about us.

The next night Mom puts an envelope on the table. "My first paycheck."

"Wow." Abby holds St. Nick to her cheek.

"What are you going to do with it?" Teddy asks.

"We'll see. Remember, this job is temporary."

There's a FOR SALE sign in our yard. Every day Dad brings home boxes and stacks them in the garage. He gave notice at work that he's leaving. This morning at breakfast he talked about buying the house in Michigan. We sat there, not speaking.

"Ma, what are we going to do?" Teddy bangs his cast on the edge of the table.

"I'm thinking," Mom says.

I bet she's thinking, Maybe this is it. He'll finally stop.

Well, Grace and I have a plan if they go. But who will help Teddy take care of Mom? What will Abby do if she wakes in the middle of the night?

"That lady you talk to, what does she say about this?" I ask.

Mom lights a cigarette. Her hands aren't shaking. Her nails are painted a soft shade of red to match her lipstick. How do I look? she asks every morning when I watch her put on her makeup.

"Mostly she just listens to me talk."

Teddy throws up his arms. "Well, what good is that?"

The back door opens, and a cool breeze follows Dad into the kitchen. When he turns toward the coffeepot, Mom sweeps the envelope into her lap where no one can see it.

Chapter 69

I don't know how to end our book. I think there should be a big dramatic scene where the robbers are captured as they're escaping. But I can't figure out how to do it. The girls are too young to capture the robbers on their own.

"Maybe they're black belts in tae kwon do," Grace says at lunch one day.

I shake my head. "I don't know. I don't want it to be too unrealistic."

After the girls escape from the cave, they could run to the sheriff for help. But it's kind of a letdown if the sheriff is the one to capture the robbers.

And I don't know what the girls should do with the reward money. Grace wants them to give it to charity. But I think they should keep it and buy an office. They need a place to go between jobs and where people can contact them about other mysteries.

"They could get someone to build a tree house," Grace says. "That would be so cool. They could lower down a ladder to anyone who wants to come up and talk."

Maybe. But a tree house isn't very safe. And what would they do in the winter? A real office would be better. With desks and chairs and maybe a couch. And a refrigerator for pop and ice cream. And a shelf full of pictures of the two of them.

Chapter 70

School is winding down. At our next-to-last newspaper meeting, Mrs. Hollis appoints me features editor for next year. Everyone congratulates me, even people I don't really know. Ariel says, "You write the best articles."

I never thought this kind of thing could happen for real. But I don't know if I'll even be here next year.

At lunch Ariel tells Roxanne, "I'm a copy editor, Grace is still on design, but Meg gets to be features editor. Usually only eighth graders get that."

"A features editor does what?" Roxanne twists her black rubber bracelets.

"Assigns features stories to everyone," Grace says. "And writes them, too."

"Great. I vote for more stories about the lovely Jennifer. Look, here she comes."

Jennifer wears a tank top, even though it's not that warm, and long, dangly earrings. She stops in front of Grace. "We're meeting at my house tomorrow to figure out what we should buy the school. Are you coming?"

She doesn't ask me, and I don't care. She's stopped saying hi. Fine.

"Sure." Grace smiles. Then Jennifer walks off.

"God, she's so annoying," Roxanne says. "It's a good thing you're helping with this. Otherwise she'd steal all our hard-earned money for herself."

"Oh, she would not," Grace says.

I dig my fists into my thighs. In front of everyone Jennifer was mean to Hannah and called her sister a pig. *Miss Piggy. Get Miss Piggy out of here!*

"Grace, you're way too nice to people," Ariel says.

"She's not so bad." Grace smiles slightly.

"Yes, she is," I say. "She's mean and selfish. And I don't understand why you'd *ever* want to be friends with her."

Grace turns away, her shoulders falling. I wish the floor would open up and swallow me.

Grace and I meet at my locker after school. We haven't spoken since lunch, even though we sat next to each other in science class. She stares at the floor as we walk.

I clench my teeth and throw my shoulders back. I was right in what I said, wasn't I? I feel a knot thicken in my throat. I should say something to fix it. But for once I've told the truth about how I feel, haven't I?

We walk slowly, heads down.

Mrs. Hollis stops us. "Meg, remind me to give you the stack of newspapers we've collected from other schools. It'll help you think of ideas over the summer."

I squeeze my eyes shut.

"Are you okay?" Mrs. Hollis asks. I'm afraid that I might cry, so I don't open my eyes. "Is it your sister?"

"She's fine."

"What's wrong with Abby?" Grace asks. I open my eyes.

Mrs. Hollis wrinkles her forehead. "I'm sorry, Meg. I assumed Grace knew."

"Knew what? Did something happen to Abby now, too?"

I'm caught in a tall tale, and I don't know how to get out of it. Mrs. Hollis looks from me to Grace. Then Grace rushes down the hall.

I catch up with her, but she walks a few steps in front of me, her arms swinging at her side.

"Wait," I say.

Finally, outside on the sidewalk, she stops and turns. Her face is red; her blue eyes are wild. "Your dad hurt Abby and you told Mrs. Hollis but you won't tell me."

"No, that's not it. Nothing happened to Abby."

"Then what was she talking about? What didn't you tell me?"

Where do I begin? For blocks and blocks I trail behind her. Why do I make up these stories, anyway? I have to do something. *Now.*

"I told Mrs. Hollis that Abby had ulcer attacks. Which she doesn't have. My family isn't from Australia and we didn't live in Tasmania and I've never had malaria."

I hold my breath.

"Those were lies?" Grace calls over her shoulder angrily.

I cringe.

I remember how Grace and I sat on her stairs during their party and looked out on Carollyn and Dr. Bennett's friends. *At least Carollyn doesn't lie to me,* Grace had said. I'm a great big liar. "I don't know why I say those things."

"What about the other stuff?" she asks. "Did you lie about that, too?"

"What other stuff?"

"That you want to be a writer. And that you think my pictures are great."

"No, of course I didn't lie about that."

"And that we're best friends. And we're always going to be best friends!"

"That's true. It is!"

We keep walking, but not speaking, until we're on the sidewalk in front of her house. She wheels around and puts her hands on her hips. Her cheeks are spotted with red blotches, and she's crying. She's angry with me for so many things.

"I'm sorry about everything," I say. "I'm sorry about what I said at lunch."

"I know Jennifer is mean. But I *won't* talk about her behind her back. Because what if it gets back to her? She'd be so hurt. Or what if something happens to her and you never, ever get a chance to say you're sorry? Think of how awful that would be!"

She turns and climbs the stairs. A shudder starts down my neck. She hates me. But I start up the stairs after her.

She's in the kitchen, her head on the counter. Carollyn stands at the sink. She tries to smile. I slip onto the stool beside Grace. Having a best friend is so new to me that I don't know how to do it very well.

"I was embarrassed." I take a deep breath. Carollyn

leaves the room. "Because everything is so wrong at my house. I didn't think you'd want to be friends with me if you knew. You have such a great family."

"My family isn't perfect." Grace keeps her head buried in her arms.

"I know, but . . ." I suck in my breath. "You know what happens when my dad drinks? He knocks things over and calls us names and picks fights. He drools down his face. Sometimes it sticks in the corner of his mouth and drips onto his shirt."

Grace looks at me, and her eyebrows squeeze together. "Why did you think I wouldn't be your friend if I knew this?"

"Because it's disgusting."

"But you're not disgusting."

We glance at each other and then look away. A pirate ship sits on the coffee table, one of Ricky's birthday presents. It's brown and black with a tall plastic mast and plastic sails. There are secret trapdoors. Little cannons. It's exactly like the one Teddy had years ago.

"You're not going to stay here, are you?" she says finally. "You're going to go."

"I don't want to go."

"If you leave, I won't have anyone to talk to anymore."

"I love my family." A sob fills my chest. "I don't know if I can leave them."

See. I knew Grace wouldn't like me if she knew everything. But that's not right. She's not angry about Dad's drinking. She's disappointed in me.

Then Ricky turns on his video game, and the phone

206

rings, and a friend of Carollyn's stops by. Grace and I sit there, looking everywhere but at each other.

But I notice that we're breathing in rhythm. In, out. In, out. In, out. I pull out the present I have for her in my backpack and leave it on the counter.

Chapter 71

Tonight we look all over the house for St. Nick, but we can't find him. Dad comes up the stairs. "He's probably halfway to Chicago by now."

"You let him out on purpose!" Abby says.

Teddy grabs his head and says, "I must have left the door open when I took out the trash."

We throw on sweatshirts. Dad laces his boots. "Let's see who finds him first." He's drunk.

Abby and Mom go to Shawna's, and Teddy and I run through the backyard. The workers have gone, but the smell of sawdust hangs in the air. We call for St. Nick and search the piles of wood, looking in the half-built houses and under piles of bricks.

I'm chilled and spooked by those big black forklifts and dump trucks towering over us. We turn on the flashlight. The stink from the foundry is so bad that I can taste it.

A half hour later we find him underneath a woodpile, scared and shivering. Teddy kneels and lays the flashlight in the dirt so it won't shine in St. Nick's face. He sweeps his hair out of his eyes and then holds out his hand and lets it rest in the dirt.

"Come here, little guy. We're here to take you home." His voice is soft and sweet.

Shouldn't we pull him out? What if Dad comes? I hear something near the dump truck and grab Teddy. But he doesn't yell at me. He keeps talking. When St. Nick finally crawls out, Teddy zips him inside his sweatshirt so only his little head shows.

Neither of us says anything on the way home, but my heart feels as if it's going to break. St. Nick totally loves and trusts Teddy. Rescuing St. Nick is the coolest thing Teddy has ever done.

Chapter 72

The next morning, Sunday, I stand in the kitchen with the phone in my hand. Grace and I haven't talked since the other day when I left her house. She's probably getting home from church right now.

When Teddy comes in, I put the phone back. Then Abby runs in. "Look! Come look!" We follow her through the backyard, past the row of houses, and along a new stretch of sidewalk. Abby screams, "Over there!"

A pair of yellow boots is stuck in the dried cement sidewalk. Next to them are footprints and a large indentation, as if someone fell.

I lean over and touch the place where the boots are cemented to the sidewalk. I run my fingers over the tomato stains on the toe. How did this happen? Dad must have stood on the sidewalk last night when we were looking for St. Nick. Then he got stuck.

"Bet he's mad that his thirty-nine ninety-five boots are ruined," Teddy says.

These boots are big and noisy when Dad clomps around in them. But they look small against the sidewalk. I sit on the warm cement.

Abby kicks off her flip-flops. "I'm going to try them."

"No." I reach for her leg. At the same time, Teddy grabs her arm. He pulls her onto his lap as he sits next to me. We stare at the boots. The sun makes the yellow canvas sparkle.

"The workers are going to have to rip up the cement," Teddy says.

"What will they do with Dad's boots?" Abby asks.

"Throw them away!" I say. "And make a new sidewalk. It'll be like this never happened."

We sit, still staring at the boots.

"Why can't I play in Dad's boots?" Abby asks. Teddy holds on to her.

"Because you don't have to," I say.

"*What?* What do you mean?"

"I don't know." I laugh and Teddy pretends to punch my arm.

I look out across the field. Cornstalks poke out of the dirt, their tops green and brown. I feel something warm shoot through my body. We have choices in our lives. This is what Dr. Bennett and Uncle Terry tried to tell me. This is how we take care of ourselves. We make choices. And change our lives.

"We have to get Mom to leave Dad." I remember how Dad smiled at me with the sun on his face that day in his truck last fall. I think about his impressions of Mr. Higgins and Fiona Wright. But I don't try to push these thoughts away. They have to stay here in my mind. The good with the bad.

"Poor Mom," Teddy says. "She doesn't deserve all this."

But when he looks at me, I don't nod. Mom has made her own choices over the years. Choices that have been pretty bad for all of us, if you ask me.

"You convince Mom," Teddy says. "She'll listen to you."

We leave the boots and walk home.

Chapter 73

That night Dad is cheerful because he's going flying. He wears new boots, all sparkly with stiff shoelaces. He tells us about the new engine he put in his plane.

"Can it still do four loops in a row?" I ask.

"It can do six, maybe more. There's so much power now. That goes to show you that you have to keep up with technology. You can't get away with stuff that's two and three years old."

He leans over the table, makes his hand into a plane, and swishes it through the air. With his eyes lit up and voice so excited, he looks like a kid. How much it must have hurt when Poppy dragged him across the floor! How scared he must have been when Poppy drank!

Who will take care of him if we leave?

After dinner I sit in the yard and look out over the cornfield and new houses. I bounce my knee and bite my cuticles. My muscles, tight along my back, begin to ache.

Dad starts up his truck and takes off down the street. When it's quiet again, I settle back into my chair. The sun has cast pink streaks across the sky. I like the way the pink plays against the blue sky and white clouds. It looks like cotton candy.

I feel so much better when Dad isn't around.

Mom finds me and pulls up a lawn chair.

"Wow," she says. "I sure haven't been paying attention. Look at how quickly those houses have gone up."

Three of the houses are bricked and roofed. The others are close behind. I feel as if I've watched these houses being built one brick at a time.

Mom still wears stockings, a green skirt, and a short-sleeve blouse. When Dad comes home from work, he can't change out of his work clothes fast enough.

"I love Dad." Something thick settles in my throat. "I can't help myself. I hate when he drinks and what he did to Teddy. But I still love him."

Mom rests her head on the back of the chair. She nods.

"In Michigan the same thing will happen all over again," I say. "He'll drink and hate his job, and he and Teddy will keep fighting. We've got to do something."

"I know," she says. "Shawna says that once you finally make the decision, it's not so hard. But, oh, I'm just . . . afraid."

I sit up. "Of what?"

"Of how hard it will be to actually do it. And how we'll survive, financially. And how he'll react. We've been married a long time. We've been like this a long time."

Like this.

"At times, when I'm talking to Shawna or my therapist or helping Dr. Bennett, I think, *We can do it*. We can go on our own. Then I come back here. I get confused."

I dig the heel of my shoe into the ground until I pull up clumps of grass and dirt.

"Dad is mean even when he's not drinking," I say. "Remember your nose? And Teddy's arm? What if he does something worse next time?"

Mom puts her hand over her mouth and shakes her head.

"You've got a job now," I say. "We could, well, we could stay with the Bennetts. That's what they told me. We could stay there until we got on our feet or something."

"Oh, they've done so much for us. We can't get them in the middle of this."

"What about staying at Shawna's?" I say, though I'm not sure. Does Mom know her well enough to ask?

"That's what she says. But their house is even smaller than ours."

I try to force the grass clumps back in place. I stand and stomp my foot on them. *Why won't they fit?* I kick my chair so hard it topples over. Mom flinches.

"Well, I'm staying," I say. "I'm not moving. I'm going to live with Grace."

Mom's mouth falls open. "You would do that? You would leave all of us? You're twelve years old!"

I stand in front of her, my hands on my hips. My mind bounces in a million directions. Still, I say, "Yes! I would. And I am! You did it, too, Mom. You left your family before. You were brave once!"

With this, Mom lowers her head. Tears roll down her cheeks when she looks back up at me. I stare at her. I'm right to say this to her. I know I am.

I pick up the lawn chair and sit. We watch the sky turn from blue and pink to gray, and then finally black.

Chapter 74

Grace and I sit together at lunch and share a microscope in science. We don't argue, but we don't talk. I want to ask her what she thought of the present I left for her.

After school she doesn't come to my locker. I sit in the library for hours and look through books about Hong Kong, and then I read about the Great Barrier Reef and the harbor in Sydney. But I don't really care about Australia anymore.

I take the long way home and come up behind our house along the cornfield. I start into the field, cutting through several rows. Grasshoppers, gnats, and flies jump out of my way. I stop and look around. The corn is nearly up to my shins now.

When we first moved here, I was surprised at how big this field was, how new and strange it felt to walk out our back door and pick a stalk of corn. Now there's nothing strange or new about it. This is what happens. Like the stink from the foundry. You get used to things. They become part of you. The good and the bad.

I met Grace and got used to being friends. What if she never forgives me? I don't think I can stand not being friends with her anymore. But if I live with her, I'll miss my family too much. And if I go to Michigan, I'll probably never see her again.

I pick up a dirt clump and squeeze it. If only Grace weren't so angry with me. But I don't miss that knot in my stomach from keeping these secrets.

As I walk toward our house, I see everyone is in the backyard, and I watch them grow taller the closer I get. Dad has lit the grill, and the charcoal nearly drowns out the smell of sawdust and stink from the foundry. Abby's boom box plays Dad's favorite radio station.

Abby points to me as I step out of the cornfield. "What are you doing in there?"

"There she is," Dad says.

He swings the spatula above his head and brings it down and stabs it in the air, like it's a sword. No one smiles or laughs. Teddy is sprawled on a lawn chair. His cast is off, and his arm is skinny and pale.

"Oh!" Dad turns up the radio and reaches for Mom. His dark hand swallows hers as he holds it to his chest. She puts up a little fight—"Bob, the hamburgers will burn"—but she laughs slightly. As she looks at Dad her eyes soften.

"What about the hamburgers?" Abby asks.

Dad spins Mom in front of us. Her skirt swings around her knees and then falls straight. They come together and dance off toward the cornfield. Dad's body blocks Mom from my view. If I didn't know she was there, I'd think he was dancing by himself.

Abby has two burgers on the spatula. Before I can tell her to stop, she flips the burgers and they fall onto the dirt.

218

"Christ!" Dad storms over. "Of all the stupid—! What are you thinking? What's the matter with you?" He shakes her. Abby's hair falls in her face, and she goes limp. Dad tries to pull her up, but she falls to the ground, sobbing.

I rush over. Teddy and Mom are right behind me.

"Leave her alone!" I scream. "Get your hands off her!"

Dad lets go. The four of us step away from him and huddle together. I look at Abby's arm for the same spidery broken blood vessels that Teddy had. Mom rubs Abby's arm gently.

"You jerk!" Teddy screams.

"What in the world is wrong with you?" Mom asks. "She was just trying to help."

"She dropped our dinner in the dirt!" His face is flushed.

Mom glares at him and pulls Abby close. She throws her shoulders back.

"You are never, ever to touch any of us, *ever again.*" Her voice is different.

"Oh, for God's sake, I didn't hurt her." Dad takes the other burgers off the grill and puts them on a paper plate. "Here, eat these."

"No."

"Take them!"

When she shakes her head, he shoves the plate in her face. A burger slides off the plate and tumbles down Mom's blouse and into the dirt. Her hands don't leave Abby and she doesn't back up. "You don't scare me anymore. And you're done tormenting us."

"Tormenting you? I don't torment you. What are you talking about?"

"You know what I'm talking about."

"You torment me! *You* make everything so hard. This is your fault."

Mom turns to Teddy and me. "Come on, I'll take you out to dinner."

"You're not leaving," he says.

"Oh, yes, we are, and you aren't going to stop us!" Her voice is louder this time, almost hysterical. I suck in my breath. "We're going to do exactly what we need to do, and you're not going to stop us. Ever."

"Who are you going to tell this time?" He laughs, but he's not smiling.

"I'll call the police and get a restraining order. And I'll tell you something else. We're not going to Michigan. We're not leaving. You're going to Michigan by yourself."

"You won't do it."

"Just watch me." She turns, and we follow her around the side of the house. Her sandals click on the driveway. When we reach her car, she leans against it. "I don't know how we'll be able to afford to stay in this house."

"Does that mean we're going with him?" Abby asks.

Mom straightens. "We'll work it out. Go get the kitten."

Chapter 75

Mom calls the Bennetts from the mall. It's dark by the time we pull up in front of Grace's house.

"Should we even be here?" Teddy asks. "Can't we go to a hotel? *Please?*"

"Hotels cost money," Mom says. "Until we work out how much we'll get from your dad, we have to be careful. Besides, Jim and I've been talking about this. We'll be here a couple of days. It'll be okay. He's going to help me find a permanent job."

Mom tries to rub the hamburger grease off her sleeve. Then she squeezes the steering wheel. I look at the house. Grace is so angry at me.

The front door opens before Mom even turns off the car. Carollyn and Dr. Bennett stand in the doorway. Have they been waiting there since Mom called? We walk up the steps and into the house. Teddy holds the kitten. Abby reaches for my hand.

I feel funny being here with my family. Part of me wants to show them how familiar I am with this place. *That lamp belonged to Grace's grandmother.* But another part of me wants to melt into the carpet. Grace stands next to the staircase. When I look at her, she smiles

221

slightly. I straighten and introduce Teddy and Abby to Dr. Bennett.

We watch TV in the den. I keep going to the door, trying to listen to what is going on in the kitchen, where Dr. Bennett, Carollyn, and Mom sit at the table. I smell coffee and occasionally hear Mom's voice. But I'm too far away to hear what they say.

Abby falls asleep on the pullout couch, St. Nick cuddled next to her. Teddy won't talk to anyone, and finally he goes to the guest room. Grace and I climb the stairs. It was easier not to worry about her with everyone else around. But now that we're alone, I think about how angry she is. She opens her door and flips on her light.

I see the present I gave her hanging above her desk. I wrote out a quote I liked from one of the books about Eleanor Roosevelt. Then I put it in a frame. This is what she wrote after her parents died: *We do not have to become heroes overnight. Just a step at a time, meeting each thing that comes up, seeing it is not as dreadful as it appeared, discovering we have the strength to stare it down.*

We sit side by side on her bed and stare at my present.

"I'm sorry," I say. "I didn't want to lie to you. I just wanted people to like me."

"You don't need to tell lies to get people to like you." She fiddles with the edge of her pillowcase. "I'm sorry, too. For all of this. And being mad."

I run my finger over the other end of the pillowcase. Grace doesn't like being mad at people, because it reminds her of when her mom died. I glance at her. She's the only friend I've ever had who knows what it's like to lose someone.

"We're not leaving," I say.

"You're not?" Grace raises her voice.

"Mom told Dad that we're not going to Michigan with him."

"Are you staying here with us?"

"I don't exactly know. But she stood up to him. For the very first time."

These words feel like chocolate syrup in my mouth. *She stood up to him. For the very first time.* I fall back on Grace's bed and close my eyes. I don't know how we'll survive or what will happen to Dad.

But I don't want to think about all that. This is where I want to be.

Chapter 76

On our last day of school, we have an end-of-the-year party in the newspaper room. We talk about summer plans. Marty is going to baseball camp. Ariel is going to her grandparents' in Wisconsin. Grace and I will work on another book, but we don't tell anyone this.

"I have news," Mrs. Hollis says. "I'm going to Africa to work on a Habitat for Humanity project. I'm so excited. I've never been there."

"Wow!" we all say.

"Meg has been there," Ariel says.

"You've been everywhere," Marty says. "Australia. India."

Everyone looks at me. I feel that familiar panic. But Grace kicks me under the table. When I look at her, she's trying to hide a smile.

"You didn't really believe those stories I told, did you?" I smile and laugh, but no one laughs back. Now what?

Marty frowns. "So your grandpa didn't really kill that shark?"

I shake my head.

"You lied about all that?" He glares and walks away. I suck in my breath.

"Meg is a writer," Grace says. "They're just stories, right? You're just trying out story material. Right? We all knew that." She laughs.

People exchange looks, and then someone wants another cupcake, and soon everyone is talking at once. But Ariel doesn't move.

I walk over to her. "It all just kind of . . . got out of control. I'm sorry."

"Oh, I knew they were made-up stories." But Ariel has dropped her eyes.

I stand there, shifting my weight. "I also made up that article about Jennifer last fall. Most of it she never said."

"Why would you do that?" Ariel snorts.

I take a deep breath. "I wanted her to like me."

Ariel jerks her head and looks at me. Finally she nods. "Well, that explains how smart she sounded."

Ariel is still upset with me. But this is truly who I am.

I look at Grace. She's licking the frosting off her third cupcake. Chocolate dots the tip of her nose. I couldn't have done this without her. This must be one of the great things about having friends. They're there when you need them, no matter what you do.

Chapter 77

Three days later we stand with Dad in the living room.

"You'll be sorry," he says to us. "You will. And it'll be too late."

He swings a duffel bag over his shoulder. His glasses are perched on the tip of his nose, and his black hair falls in his face. Over the past three days he has gone from being angry to begging us not to leave him. Today he's somewhere in between.

"You and your fancy friends and lawyers and therapists," Dad says.

"Be happy that I didn't call Child Protective Services and tell them that you broke your son's arm," Mom says. "Then you would have gone to jail."

Dad scowls, but he doesn't move. How different everything is, with this threat we hold over him. And now that other people know.

Abby and I hug him. Teddy folds his arms across his chest and stays where he is. So does Mom. "I don't know when I'll see you again," he says.

"I told you," Mom says. "We'll figure everything out."

He leaves. I watch him through the screen as he hurls his bag into his truck. The back of the truck is filled with things from his workshop. Planes. His favorite chair.

"I don't think I can breathe." Mom is crying and holding herself. My heart begins to race. "I don't know how we're going to do this."

Teddy takes a step toward her.

Dad starts his truck. I turn. The taillights go on. I bolt out the door. *"Wait!"*

I stop at the driver's side, and he rolls down the window halfway.

He glances at me with his sad eyes and then looks out the windshield. Last fall when I sat next to him in the truck, I wanted to hold on to something. I wanted to find his good side. Maybe I'm more like Grace than I realized. Because I still love him. He'll always be my dad.

"Did you bring coffee?" I ask. He likes his coffee black, every day, all day long.

"No. I couldn't take the coffeemaker."

I feel guilty that we're keeping it. I should go get it. I glance at Abby, Mom, and Teddy in the window. But I don't move. I look at his hands. His fingers are big and wide and covered with thick black hair. They are steady as they rest on the steering wheel.

"Maybe that house where you're renting a room will have a coffeemaker."

"Maybe, but maybe not."

I feel something pull inside me. He looks like a boy, like Mr. Higgins, and like my dad all at the same time. Maybe he feels the same way, as if he's all these people. I wonder if we've done the right thing. If I have done the right thing.

"Well, I better go," he says.

"I love you, Dad." I put my hands on the window. I don't want him to go.

He nods and puffs out his lip. He looks out the windshield and turns back to me.

"You take care of yourself," he says. "You keep doing good in school, okay?"

I nod. He puts the truck in gear, and I step back.

"This isn't going to be forever," he says. "We'll be together again. You just wait."

I follow him as he backs up. Then I watch as he slowly drives away. When the road curves and I can no longer see his truck, I sit on the curb. It's quiet now, except for the birds and the faint voices of the workers in the new houses. I stretch my feet out in front of me and tap my toes together.

When I look back at the house, I feel a little thrill start up my back. Tonight we'll have dinner and we won't worry about Dad.

We won't have to wait for him to see how we'll be.

I glance down the street where Dad disappeared and see someone coming toward me. It's Grace on her bike. She stops, puts down her kickstand, and sits down next to me on the curb. "He's gone?"

"Yep."

"Are you okay?"

"I told him I love him." I don't know if I can tell Mom and Teddy and Abby about this. I look at Grace. Her blond hair is pulled back in a ponytail. The tip of her nose is red and peeling. We both got sunburns at the lake yesterday. She stretches out her legs so that our feet are side by side.

"I wish I'd told my mom that." Grace drops her eyes.

Our knees are the same round, bumpy shape. "She knew."

Grace raises her eyebrows and nods. "What do you want to do?"

I think about Emily and Samantha and how I still don't have an ending for our book. But now I have a new book idea. "Maybe Emily discovers that her grandfather was this hero in Australia. Then they'll go there to solve another mystery."

"Yeah, and they go diving off the Great Barrier Reef," she says. "The fish are supposed to be really colorful. That would be cool to draw."

"Someone is trying to drill for oil on the reef and it's threatening to destroy it."

"And the girls save the reef and take the reward money and give it to poor kids."

I smile and so does Grace. I look at my toes again.

How will I end the book I'm still writing? But maybe it doesn't matter who eventually captures the robbers or what the girls do with the reward money.

What's important to them is that they saved each other's lives.

And then I think, *Grace has saved my life*. And this may be the best feeling I've ever had.

Acknowledgments

Many thanks to my agent, Amy Jameson, and my editor, Wendy Lamb, for having faith in me, and to Ruth Homberg, Annie Kelley, and Andrew Bast at Random House for their help. Also to Mitali Perkins and my critique group for great advice. And to Kathy Read for being a good friend and for reading every single draft. Thanks especially to David for always believing.

About the Author

Karen Day grew up in Indiana and now lives in Newton, Massachusetts, with her husband and their three children. Her love of reading and writing has taken her through careers in journalism and teaching. She is also the author of *No Cream Puffs*. You can visit Karen at www.klday.com.